He watched as her gaze drifted to the watch on her delicate wrist and saw the sign that she was thinking about leaving.

Something he knew he didn't want her to do.

Her lips parted, no doubt to bid her farewells. Not wanting the evening to end just yet, Diego reached out, placing his hand over hers while obscuring the watch. Her skin was soft under his hand, radiating heat into him that turned into a fiery spark when it penetrated his skin.

"How long are you staying in Rio?" he asked and noticed a strange huskiness coating his voice. Like he wanted her to stay longer. Which was ridiculous because one night was all anyone ever got with him, so it didn't matter how long she planned on staying.

Ana looked at him with wide eyes, as if feeling the same intense spark jumping between them when he'd first touched her. She twisted her hand so that their palms were now touching, the tips of her fingers grazing over the inside of his hand.

"Only tonight."

Dear Reader,

Thank you for choosing to read *Her Secret Rio Baby*. I'm excited I get to share Eliana and Diego's story, which is close to my heart because it's set in Brazil and celebrates and highlights Latin characters and their lives.

The first version of this story was fueled by coffee and cake as I sat in my kitchen with the real Ana. I was stuck, you see. I knew who Diego and Eliana were, but I didn't know how to get from where they are to where I envisioned them to be. A lot of obscure and outrageous ideas later and their story and journey started to take shape.

Eliana struggled with her sense of belonging her entire life, not knowing who to call her people or where to find them. She returns to Rio de Janeiro to deal with her father's estate.

And runs straight into Diego, who knows exactly who his people are and goes to great lengths to do right by his community.

It's that sense of community I'm so excited for you to read about.

Luana <3

HER SECRET
RIO BABY

———

LUANA DAROSA

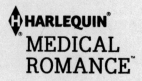

HARLEQUIN®
MEDICAL
ROMANCE™

Recycling programs
for this product may
not exist in your area.

ISBN-13: 978-1-335-73736-6

Her Secret Rio Baby

Copyright © 2022 by Luana DaRosa

All rights reserved. No part of this book may be used or reproduced in any manner whatsoever without written permission except in the case of brief quotations embodied in critical articles and reviews.

This is a work of fiction. Names, characters, places and incidents are either the product of the author's imagination or are used fictitiously. Any resemblance to actual persons, living or dead, businesses, companies, events or locales is entirely coincidental.

For questions and comments about the quality of this book, please contact us at CustomerService@Harlequin.com.

Harlequin Enterprises ULC
22 Adelaide St. West, 41st Floor
Toronto, Ontario M5H 4E3, Canada
www.Harlequin.com

Printed in U.S.A.

Once at home in sunny Brazil, **Luana DaRosa** has since lived on three different continents, though her favorite romantic location remains the tropical places of Latin America. When she's not typing away at her latest romance novel or reading about love, Luana is either crocheting, buying yarn she doesn't need or chasing her bunnies around her house. She lives with her partner in a cozy town in the south of England. Find her on Twitter under the handle @ludarosabooks.

Books by Luana DaRosa

Harlequin Medical Romance

Falling for Her Off-Limits Boss

Visit the Author Profile page at Harlequin.com.

For the real Ana, thank you
for being an amazing friend.

CHAPTER ONE

When Eliana came down to the hotel bar she hadn't planned on meeting anyone. Especially not the out-of-this-world-handsome man sitting on the barstool one over from her. While catching up on the *futebol* game she hadn't noticed him sit down, until he struck up a conversation about the new manager of one of the teams. Something that threw her off. Men usually assumed she knew nothing about the sport.

At first glance he seemed no more than a well-dressed businessman finding refuge at the bar after a long day. But the longer she kept looking at him, the more her skin tingled below the surface as the extent of his devastating handsomeness coalesced in her mind.

His suit was tailored to perfection, clinging to his body as if he had been born in it. The fabric was the kind of black that swallowed a man not confident enough to wear it. Not him. He dominated every fibre with a quiet but electric sensuality.

The only thing that seemed out of place in this vision was the charcoal-black shoulder-length hair that had been carelessly ruffled on one side to keep it out of his face. Eliana wanted to dig her fingers through the strands of that hair and tug him closer to her.

The fantasy came over her unbidden, intruding on her already exposed nerves, and she shook her head. It must be her tired brain, she told herself as she bit the inside of her cheek to stop herself from licking her lips as she noticed his eyes dart to them for a fraction of a second.

Eliana had spent the better part of her day travelling from Belo Horizonte to Rio de Janeiro. A bereavement had brought her here. Her father Marco, along with her half-brother Vanderson, had died in an accident a couple of days ago. A fact that had left her numb on the inside.

She had never been close to either of them—hadn't even attended their funeral. A part of her had wanted to…to take that final opportunity to say goodbye to the only family she'd had left. But when it had come to it she'd backed out, staying locked in her hotel room as she got to grips with the new reality she now lived in.

She was now the heiress to her father's hospital and fortune, and that was a twist of fate no one had seen coming—Eliana least of all.

'May I?' the man asked, pointing at the empty barstool between them.

Eliana nodded, taking a big sip of her wine as he slipped into the seat. She could almost feel the heat of his body radiating towards her. They were discussing last night's *futebol* match, yet her body was reacting as if he had whispered tantalising words into her ear.

She glanced at her wristwatch. It was late enough not to seem impolite if she left. Her flight was early the next day, and today had already been long and tedious. Going now would save her a lot of energy she didn't have.

Except Eliana didn't want to leave. Not really. The man's casual banter had made her forget about her heavy heart for a moment, and the way his dark eyes looked her over ignited small fires all over her skin.

It was a reaction she didn't expect, but one that also wasn't entirely unwelcome. This was what people did, right? They met in bars, decided to have some fun.

'I'm Diego,' he said, and it was only then she realised she had been staring at him.

His name sent a cascade of heat down her spine. He had only introduced himself. Why did it feel as if he just said something dirty to her?

'Ana,' she replied and took his outstretched hand. His grip was firm, and his fingers grazed her skin for just a moment as he held onto her hand a flash longer than was necessary.

A spark appeared at the spot where he'd broken their physical connection, travelling down her arm before settling in the pit of her stomach.

'What brings you to Rio?'

A smile curled the full lips, highlighting the distinguished features of his face even more. He wore his jacket open, the linen shirt visible beneath giving her an idea of the pure masculine fantasy hidden underneath the fabric. A thought that dominated her to the point where she had to remind herself that they were in the middle of a conversation.

She'd been a woman at a bar before, talking to men like Diego. But she couldn't remember ever having such an instant and visceral reaction to anyone's proximity.

'The funeral of my father.'

She didn't want to discuss her father with anyone, but she needed something to distract herself from the fire eating her insides. He didn't need to know she hadn't gone.

'I'm sorry to hear that.' Diego's face softened.

'Don't be. We weren't close.' Eliana tried to keep the bitter edge out of her voice as much as she could. But the words tumbled out of her mouth before she could think better of it.

To her surprise, Diego scoffed and took a sip of his drink. 'I know what that's like.'

'Ah, we have father problems in common?'

His eyes darted to hers, darkening as their gazes meshed. A shiver crawled through her as she glimpsed a hint of the vulnerability he must keep hidden away behind his detached facade. The moment only lasted a second, before shutters fell over his eyes, cutting her off from anything that lay beyond the surface.

Which was just as well. Eliana wasn't looking for any attachment here in Rio. The complexity of her father's estate meant she'd need to briefly come back in a month, to claim the hospital and wrap up anything else that needed to be done to have Marco Costa out of her life for ever. She hoped to see as little of Rio de Janeiro as possible. The city bore nothing but nightmares for her.

Diego shrugged her question off, shifting his attention from his own contemplations to her. His pupils were dilated as his eyes darted back to her mouth. A signal that sent fire licking across her skin.

She wasn't imagining the crackling air between them. At least not if she trusted the signs she'd noticed.

'I see how it is. It's fine for me to reveal my secrets, but you won't tell me any of yours.' She took a sip of her drink. Her gaze locked into his. 'I'm always going to be a stranger you met at a bar. What do you have to lose?'

Eliana wasn't sure why she was prying. Under normal circumstances she never would. But Diego intrigued her. Their conversation so far had already differed from the usual bar flirting she knew. Instead of asking about her life or her job, he'd found a common interest to talk about.

Did that mean he wanted to get to know her better?

The thought gave her pause. Hotel bar flirtations weren't the romances one read about in novels. Besides, such a concept had no place in her life right now.

'Why spoil the evening?' He smiled—only half sincere—but even that was enough to bring heat to her cheeks.

In a defeated gesture, Eliana raised her hands. 'Have it your way, *senhor*, but then I get to know something else. Tell me what brought *you* to Rio instead.'

He relaxed against the bar, with one arm resting on top of it while the other hand came up to his face, scrubbing over the light stubble covering his gorgeous high cheekbones.

'Would you believe me if I said the funeral of my brother?'

He wasn't *really* his brother. There had been no blood relation between him and Vanderson. But, despite Diego having ten siblings, he'd felt closer to that man than to any of his actual relatives.

He'd met Vanderson Costa when they were both eighteen and starting their mandatory military service in the Brazilian army. They'd both signed up for the medical training, their eyes set on med school after their service concluded.

Under normal circumstances the two would never have met. Vanderson had lived in a mansion in Ipanema, Rio's most luxurious neighbourhood, while Diego himself had grown up on the outskirts of Complexo do Alemão, one of the largest slums north of the city centre. But during their service they'd all been recruits, brothers-in-arms going through it all together. Their friendship had bridged the gap in wealth and privilege, teaching Diego so much about himself and his path in life.

And now Vanderson was dead.

Losing his chosen brother clung to his heart as if someone had tied heavy weights to his chest when the news had reached him. To his surprise, he realised that this moment was the first during which he felt he could breathe easier again.

Somehow, this woman sitting in front of him was part of that process.

Diego had lived in Rio de Janeiro his entire life, and the only reason he found himself in a hotel was Vanderson's funeral. He'd attended a small dinner with the surviving family—Vanderson's husband and daughter.

He'd been about to leave when the woman sitting alone at the bar had caught his attention. Red undertones wove themselves through her dark brown hair, which flowed in lavish curls over her shoulders and looked silken to the touch. But what had drawn him in more than her hair, and the sensual curves visible even while she was sitting down, was what she'd been doing. She'd been looking at a nearby TV, watching the sports pundits who were discussing last night's *futebol* game.

Being a *futebol* enthusiast himself, he had felt his interest piqued enough for him to walk over and see what she was doing.

Though Diego hadn't been as subtle as he'd thought, and a few moments after he'd sat down she'd turned her head to look at him. Time had stopped for several heartbeats when their gazes collided, and he'd experienced an unusual twinge in his chest. He'd tried to look nonchalant—as if he hadn't checked her out—but his body had refused to take any orders.

The light brown hue of her eyes was mesmerising. Every now and again the light hit her irises just right, giving them the appearance of pure gold.

She clearly didn't understand the beauty she possessed. He could see that in the way she held herself. More than that, though, her analytical mind and quick wit had jumped out at him when they'd discussed the game. It spoke of passion, and he wanted to get to know her better, to understand what other areas of her life this passion unfolded into.

Which was a strange thought in itself. Diego never got to know the women who entered his life. It wasn't anything personal, and he was upfront about it. He had watched his parents destroy themselves in the name of love, and knew the path of a romantic relationship only led to pain and forced sacrifices.

Diego made sure he got out before things got too emotional and involved. And one way to avoid all that was by not asking too many questions before moving on to the key event of the evening.

So why was he sitting here, asking about her relationship with her father? Or even telling her why he had come here?

Ana's eyes narrowed as she looked him over, a slight frown pulling the corners of her mouth downwards. 'Interesting how this bar is collecting the bereaved.' She paused for a moment. 'I'm sorry to hear about your brother.'

He smiled, feeling the sincerity of her sympathy radiate a gentle warmth through his skin. 'Life is going to suck without him.'

Diego allowed himself to feel the truth of his

words with this virtual stranger he found himself drawn to.

He watched as her eyes drifted to the watch on her delicate wrist and saw the signs that she was thinking about leaving. Something he knew he didn't want her to do.

Her lips parted, no doubt to bid him farewell. Not wanting the evening to end just yet, Diego reached out, placing his hand over hers while obscuring the watch. Her skin was soft under his hand, radiating more heat into him that turned into a fiery spark as it penetrated his skin.

'How long are you staying in Rio?' he asked, and noticed a strange huskiness coating his voice. As if he wanted her to stay. Which was ridiculous. Because one night was all anyone ever got with him, so it didn't matter how long she planned on staying.

Ana looked at him with wide eyes. Was she feeling the same intense spark jumping between them when he touched her? She twisted her hand so that their palms were touching, the tips of her fingers grazing over the inside of his hand.

'Only tonight.'

She hesitated for a moment, and Diego saw the wheels behind her eyes turning. There was something she wanted to tell him. For a moment he held his breath in anticipation, but then the light in her eyes dimmed and she remained quiet.

Ana didn't know her assumption about him being from out of town was wrong. He hadn't corrected her. The information was irrelevant. Tomorrow she would be back wherever she came from, while he would be left alone to contemplate a new reality where his best friend was no more.

He hadn't been able to stop himself when he'd seen Ana. Her presence seemed soothing, and it had required only one bat of her long lashes to awaken a roaring fire in his chest. He knew this reaction was different...unlike the usual flings he satisfied himself with. But he didn't care in this moment. His pain faded when that flame spread through his body. He planned on feeding it until exhaustion took him.

'Then I'm glad I spotted you when I did, or I might have missed the opportunity of a lifetime, Donna Ana.'

'You sat down at the bar because you saw me?'

Scepticism laced her voice, and Diego almost laughed at that. There was no way a gorgeous woman like her didn't have men approaching her in bars all the time. Yet she seemed surprised.

'Couldn't help it,' he replied, his voice dropping low as he wove his fingers through hers.

While his mind was still trying to decide his body had taken control, reacting to the attraction arcing between them.

Eliana's heart slammed against her ribcage as Diego's fingers wrapped around her hand, giving it a gentle squeeze. The brown-green hue of his eyes darkened as the attraction that had been whirring around them for the last hour became almost tangible. Their hands touching had created a rapturous reaction within her, and her breath had caught in her throat. How was this even possible?

'An unlikely story,' she said, not able to keep her scepticism at bay.

She knew he was using honeyed words to flirt with her, and yet she couldn't stop the chemicals firing in her brain. Their connection was an intense physical sensation, clawing its way throughout her body.

'You don't believe that I had no choice once I saw you?'

His voice vibrated low, seeping through her pores and into her body, settling behind her belly button with an uncomfortable pinch.

'I think that's a phrase you came up with and that it has proved most successful with all the different women you meet at bars.'

The words rang with the sound of an accusation although she hadn't meant it.

Diego had clearly picked up on the subtle nuance as well, for he arched one of his eyebrows. 'What do you think I'm after?'

His fingers were still entwined with hers, and the tips of them were rubbing against the back of her hand, sending sparkling showers across her arm. Heat rose through her body, entangling itself with the knot his touch had tied in her stomach and colliding with the sparks that were descending through her arm.

Everything about him made her react. He was like a potent magnet drawing at the fibres of her body. Control had slipped from her hands, and Eliana needed to regain it. She wasn't the type of person to let it go that easily. But Diego was shrouding her thoughts in the thick mists of an instant attraction that was unlike any she had ever experienced before.

'You want to sleep with me.' No use beating around the bush.

'Ah, straight to the point. Do you really want to skip the witty back-and-forth?'

His lips parted in a devastating grin, and Eliana caught her breath for a moment.

'I've been told I'm a pretty good flirt,' he said.

She chuckled at the aura of confidence he exuded, not wanting to let him know how deeply it impacted on her. 'I'm sure that's what they've all told you.'

Her words had the desired effect, for Diego took his free hand to clasp his chest with an indignant expression on his face. 'You wound me, Donna Ana. You're not wrong with your assessment, but I make sure a woman feels worshipped and cherished above anything else.'

Eliana raised a delicate eyebrow, thrown off guard by his bluntness. It matched hers, so she shouldn't be surprised the way she was. His fingers wrapped around hers were creating a luscious fog around her, draping her in a cloud charged with desire and passion.

It made her wonder what else he could do with his fingers if this innocent touch had already raised all the hair along her arms. The soft curve of his lips begged to be kissed… She wanted to lose herself in the delicious promise they wrote on his face.

'What is your usual plan of seduction?'

Maybe she didn't want to skip all the foreplay. Eliana was still telling herself that she wasn't in his thrall, that she could step back at any moment. But the flames of desire uncoiling themselves in her chest had already surrendered to his charms. She wanted *all* of him.

'Normally I would buy you some drinks, and show my appreciation for your taste in alcohol. We'd discuss some unimportant things about our lives, and I would grab at every opportunity to flatter you. Touch you here and there as you tell me about yourself...'

Diego got up and stepped closer to her, forcing her to tilt her head up so she could look at him. His hand wandered up to her exposed arm, touching her shoulder before slipping down, leaving a series of fires under her skin.

'I don't like to talk about myself that much,' she told him. Her voice sounded husky, and she was enthralled by the pure masculine magnetism he exuded. He could have her right this second if he asked.

He dipped his head, his face so close to hers now that the smell of his aftershave drifted up her nose. The scent of moss and earth shrouded her thoughts in an even more alluring mist, and without giving it a second thought she leaned in closer, wanting to close the gap between them.

'Well, it's a good thing you've already figured me out, so we can skip that part, can't we?' Diego whispered in a deep voice filled with promises of desire.

He shifted his head further, his lips grazing her ear and sending a sensual shiver down her spine.

No, would be the correct answer. But why? After the stress of this day, a bit of comfort in the arms of an otherworldly handsome man would be a soothing balm for her battered nerves. He'd made it clear that this was what he did, so there wouldn't be any feelings hurt. And from the way he'd wrapped her around his little finger from the very beginning, she knew it would be *good*. What harm could one night do?

Eliana grabbed her bag before getting off the stool and stepping closer. Her hand trailed down his arm as she leaned in, so her lips brushed against his skin in a small suggestion of a kiss as she whispered, 'I'm in Room 901. Finish your drink and meet me upstairs in fifteen minutes.'

CHAPTER TWO

DIEGO'S NIGHT HAD been restless. He'd thought sleep would come easier now, more than a month after Vanderson's funeral, but rest still eluded him now and then. Sometimes it was due to grief, but more often than not worry kept him awake at night. Worry about the future and the low hum of an unmet need stirring in his chest.

Ana.

The beautiful stranger he'd met at a bar.

He had followed her to her room that night four weeks ago, where he'd had the best sex of his entire life. So good he still remembered how her body had felt on top of him. They had fitted together as if they were made for each other.

That thought kept crawling back into his mind, and Diego had to shake it. They were most definitely *not* made for each other. What had possessed him even to think that? They'd spent the night together and enjoyed an explosive connection. There was no need to attach more meaning to it.

But he wanted more. More of someone he couldn't have. Diego didn't know how to *give* more. His parents had made sure of that. Their constant betrayal of one another had taught him that love only made people do foolish things. He would rather stay single for ever than risk doing to a woman what his father had done to his mother.

His eyelids still heavy with the lack of sleep, Diego threw on some grey scrubs and flipped the switch on the coffee machine in the kitchen. He left the room through the glass door leading outside, crossing a small patch of grass and entering the garage next to his house. He squinted when he flipped on the light, his senses still awakening after his poor sleep.

Instead of a car and other household items, the garage was filled with medical and sports equipment. A big workbench stood on the far side of the room, with a prosthetic limb on top of it.

With a heavy sigh falling from his lips, Diego approached the bench to look at the small leg he had spent most of his free time on in the last week. He was supposed to be fitting it to its owner, a young boy who had visited him last month with a request for a new leg as he had outgrown his old one.

It wasn't often that Diego found patients who needed prosthetics visiting him in the free clinic he ran in Complexo do Alemão. The average person sought him out for the kind of maladies any general practitioner could take care of, as well as wounds that needed stitching. His expertise as an orthopaedic surgeon wasn't called upon very often.

Diego never refused a patient—sometimes at significant personal cost. But he remembered all too well what it had been like growing up in that area, devoid of any kind of hope for a better future. He had escaped his life of poverty, relying on tenacity and just the right amount of luck. And that last thing—along with his memories of his time in the slums—inspired him to work hard and give back to his community.

'Is this the leg for Miguel? I've just seen his mother at your sister's shop, and she told me about it.'

Diego jumped at the sudden voice behind him and spun around. His grandmother, Márcia, had come into the garage with a small tray that held a cup of coffee and some pieces of toast.

'Avozinha, what are you doing here so early?' he asked as he approached her, taking the tray out of her hands and kissing her on the cheek in greeting.

'Pelé likes to be out in the morning, so we took a walk here to check in on you.'

Diego looked past his grandma and into the garden. A large greyhound was sniffing around the grass, lifting his long snout when Diego whistled and bolting towards him with an excited yelp.

Diego went down on one knee and scratched Pelé's throat. The tags around his collar gave a soft jingle as he rubbed his hands up and down the neck of the animal.

'Wait, you went all the way to Aline's shop? You shouldn't walk in that neighbourhood on your own.'

He looked up at Márcia, who frowned, flipping her hand in a throwaway gesture. 'I'm not alone. Pelé looks after me.'

'This little coward? Remember when you had a trespasser in your garden and he hid under the coffee table when he noticed a stranger? He is cute, but that won't save you.'

Diego smoothed the light brown fur flat with one last pat and then rubbed the greyhound between his large, trusting eyes before he lifted himself off the ground to face his grandmother.

'Don't you lecture me on where I can and cannot go, young man. I've looked out for you since you were knee-high and see what you've become.'

Diego tried his best not to roll his eyes as Márcia went for her favourite topic: her surgeon grandson and how she had saved him from ending up on the street mixed up with the wrong crowd. If he was honest with himself, she did deserve all the credit. She had taken it upon herself to raise him when his parents had been too busy sorting themselves out.

'*Sim,* Vovo. You know I worry about you,' he said and raised his hands in defeat. He could never defeat her in a duel of words.

'You'd better worry about Miguel. He needs a new leg.'

Diego turned around with a frustrated grunt, looking back at his workbench and the prosthetic limb that was giving him such a hard time. 'I didn't expect to be doing it on my own. Vanderson had agreed to let me borrow some time from the paediatric specialist on my team.'

'What about Marco's daughter? She will be the new owner, yes? Maybe she won't be against you helping Miguel.'

He turned around to look at his grandmother, a sceptical eyebrow raised. 'I don't know what to expect from her. She and the Costas weren't even on speaking terms for the last seventeen years. Vanderson told me she's a doctor, too. But his father wouldn't let him have any contact with her.'

Diego shook his head. This wasn't just about him needing hospital resources to help one patient. The free clinic he ran whenever time permitted required more support than he could provide on his own. Even if he could hire just one nurse to work there during the daytime,

he would be able to help so many more people.
But to do that he needed the help of the chief
of medicine at Santa Valeria Hospital. A role
that had belonged to Marco Costa until his re-
cent death.

Eliana Oliveira. That was her name. The
word in the corridors of Santa Valeria was that
she would arrive any day now, to assume the
position as chief of medicine.

Outside of the scandal surrounding her birth,
no one knew much about her. She was a complete unknown to Diego, who had a lot more
than just his staff at the hospital to worry about.
He planned on getting the leg sorted out for the
little boy Miguel with or without approval from
the new chief. Though he'd prefer to do it with
her blessing.

'I'm sure she'll be reasonable,' Márcia said,
and patted his arm with a reassuring smile.

He wished he could share her optimism about
the new chief, but he'd rather prepare for the
worst and be surprised.

With a sigh, Diego glanced at his phone's display to check the time, grabbing the toast his
avozinha had made for him.

'I'd better go. I don't want to be late if today
is the day she actually bothers to show up.'

Eliana sat behind the opulent desk that stood in
the chief's office—formerly inhabited by her es-

tranged father—and her stomach roiled again, making her hand fly to her mouth. The stress of being back in Rio de Janeiro to deal with the administration of the Santa Valeria General Hospital was taking a lot more out of her than she had expected. She had woken up from an uneasy slumber with nausea cascading through her in violent waves as she'd tried her best to look presentable for the day.

Suelen, the assistant to the chief of medicine, had given her a diary with all her appointments for the day. Ten people wanted to speak to her today, all of them about an important matter—according to them. Eliana doubted any of them were as urgent as they made them out to be.

Leaning back in the chair, she let her head fall back and closed her eyes for a moment, willing the next wave of nausea away.

She was nervous, and her body was reacting to the tension. She was meant to be a consultant—not the chief. Her training as a general surgeon had not prepared her for all the administrative work she was now expected to do. All the different reports on financial matters only worsened her already troubled stomach.

It was only going to be for a couple of weeks, she told herself as she scrubbed her hands over her face. She would pick a new chief of medicine to do the job for her and go back to Belo Horizonte. Rio held nothing but old pain for her, and she didn't want to be here. Hell, she didn't even want to be the owner of this hospital.

People who had known her father might think she had followed in his footsteps going into the medical field. He had been the prestigious hospital's owner, after all. But he'd only played a small part in her motivation.

Her mother was the one she wanted to be like. She had been a nurse at Santa Valeria when she'd got pregnant. Her parents had been having an affair, and instead of stepping up and assuming responsibility her father had driven her mother out of town so no one would learn about his infidelity.

Time and again Marco Costa had shown himself to be a dishonourable man, and Eliana wanted nothing to do with anything that had once belonged to the man. Not when he had broken her mother so wholly that she hadn't been able to hang on to life. She could almost hear the whispers of the older staff—the ones who had known her mother and what Marco Costa had done to her.

But life rarely considered what someone wanted, so despite her quite visceral opposition in this matter she now had to deal with the inheritance her father had left her. The day she heard his name for the last time couldn't come soon enough.

'Excuse me, Dr Oliveira?'

Her head snapped back to its original position when she heard the knock, followed by the soft voice of her assistant.

Eliana cleared her throat, swallowing the bile she felt rising in it. 'Is it already time for my first appointment?' she asked, glancing at her schedule.

'Ah, no...' Suelen hesitated for a fraction before speaking again. 'A registrar in general surgery has called for help. There are some complications with a surgery, and none of the other consultants seem to be available.'

Her words made Eliana blink slowly for a couple of seconds, unable to comprehend what she had just said. 'There are no consultants to help the junior surgeons? Where are they?'

Suelen looked down at her notepad, a faint blush streaking over her cheeks. She was clearly uncomfortable with the answer. 'It seems one of them called in sick, three are stuck in their own surgeries, and another two are...' she looked down to check her notes again '...playing golf.'

'What?' Eliana got up from her chair and waved the assistant to come with her. 'Move my meetings around. I'll take care of it myself. Just show me to the OR.'

Despite the nerves flipping her stomach inside out, Eliana felt an odd excitement rise within her at the thought of stepping into the

OR. That, at least, was a world she understood and felt comfortable in.

They rushed to the general surgery wing, where Suelen pointed her towards OR Three. Eliana wasted no time scrubbing in as fast as she could, and thanked the OR nurse when she stepped out into the scrub room to greet her.

'Do you have a pair of spare shoes around?' she asked the nurse, glancing down at the high heels she was wearing. 'Anything will be a vast improvement.'

'I think we have some *chinelas* for such cases here.' The woman bent down, opening a small cupboard and rummaging around before pulling out a pair of neon green slippers.

Eliana stared at them for a moment, as if she was facing off a venomous snake. They really couldn't have been less flattering if they'd tried. 'Well, I did say anything would be better,' she said with a laugh as she kicked her heels off and stowed them in the cupboard the nurse had just pulled the slippers from.

She received a gown and gloves with a smile, tying a mask around the back of her head as she readied herself to help the surgeon. The doors to the operations room opened with a familiar sound, and a sense of control enveloped her, calming her rioting stomach.

Eliana stepped up to the patient and watched

as the registrar struggled to keep the surgical field clear.

'What happened?' she asked, her voice calm. For the first time today, she felt as if she knew exactly what was happening.

'Blunt force trauma caused a tear in the diaphragm. When we went in we found unexpected damage to the kidneys as well. There was a lot more blood than we had expected.' The panicked registrar looked around at her colleague. 'The consultant was supposed to be with us, but we had no time to wait.'

'It's all right. I'm here to help.' Eliana stepped closer to the patient. 'First we want to isolate the bleeding. Clamp, please.' Eliana stretched out her hand and a moment later the cold steel of the instrument hit her gloved palm.

'I think there must be a rupture on one kidney.'

Hesitation was mixed with despair in the doctor's voice and it made Eliana frown behind her mask. They must have spent a lot of time looking for a superior while the situation was unfolding.

She nodded to reassure her. There was no room for panic in the operating room. 'Yes, blunt force trauma strong enough to hurt the diaphragm like that can cause damage to the kidneys as well. Let's clamp the renal artery to see if the bleeding subsides.'

Looking down at the patient, Eliana pointed out the artery in question and placed a clamp there.

'Suction here so we can see better,' she instructed the other junior surgeon, who moved the instrument to where she had indicated.

The visibility on the kidneys soon cleared and a lot less blood was replacing the stuff they suctioned away.

'Good. Always isolate the source of bleeding by clamping the right artery. Now we can work on the repair unobstructed.'

With the blood flow stemmed, they could focus on repairing the damage.

'I think this should be familiar territory for you. What are the next steps?'

The junior surgeon looked at her before dropping her eyes back to the patient.

Eliana listened to her instructions, nodding as the surgeon explained the next steps.

Her hands were itching to grab the scalpel herself. It had been some time since she'd performed any kind of surgery. After earning her general surgeon's classification she'd been asked by her teaching hospital to stay on as a consultant—which she'd agreed to do, with a request for a sabbatical so she could have a break after studying for her board certification.

A break that she had only been able to enjoy

for a few days before the news of her father's accident had reached her.

But even with her desire to work on the patient herself Eliana took the opportunity to talk the two junior surgeons through the procedure rather than do it. If these junior staff had been empowered to make their own decisions to begin with, maybe they wouldn't have been so lost in what she considered a rather common complication in a case such as this one.

Eliana repressed a sigh behind her mask, pushing the thought away and focusing on the task in front of her. This was only her first day, and she was already uncovering things that would threaten to extend her stay in Rio de Janeiro when she wanted nothing else but to leave this place behind.

Diego had just left a patient's room when his phone vibrated with a page. The nurses' station in the general surgery wing were asking him to report to their department on an urgent matter. He furrowed his brow, unsure what that meant. As the head of the orthopaedics department, he rarely dealt with anyone outside of his own staff.

He hesitated, staring at the screen of his phone. Something wasn't right. His staff had told him that the new chief of medicine had arrived today. Did it have something to do with her? The orthopaedics head nurse had told him Chief Oliveira had requested a meeting with him next week.

Putting his phone back into his pocket, he hurried towards the general surgery wing and stopped at the nurses' station, looking at the man standing behind it. 'What happened? I got an urgent page to come here.'

The nurse nodded with a heavy sigh. 'Thank you, Dr Ferrari. I didn't know who else to page in this situation. None of the consultants answered my call, and I have two very nervous junior surgeons freaking out in OR Three.'

Diego glanced at the whiteboard with the surgical schedule written on it. There were four surgeries scheduled for right now, with two additional consultants on floor duties.

'Where are those two?' He nodded towards the whiteboard.

This time the nurse rolled his eyes. 'You know them… They were Dr Costa's lackeys and they won't lift a single finger if no one makes them. They made themselves such a cosy nest over the years, they don't know how to do actual work any more.'

Diego had to suppress a sigh at that. Unfortunately for him, and the entire hospital, not every doctor in the building had the work ethic he considered essential. In fact, quite a few of the higher-ranking doctors were friends and associates of the former chief of medicine, and that was exactly the way they acted around the hospital. As if they were untouchable and not bound by the rules everyone else was following.

But now was not the time to think about that. 'You said OR Three?' he asked.

The nurse nodded, but his gaze shifted slightly, as if he was trying to decide whether he should say something more.

Diego arched his brow in a silent question.

'We paged you ten minutes ago. The registrars were freaked out. We weren't sure whether you were coming, so we had to page someone else.' There was mild apprehension in his voice.

'Who did you page?'

'The chief. She came down straight away, so I think they should be done by now. Though I haven't seen them leave the OR yet...'

Diego couldn't keep the surprise out of his expression. It seemed Marco Costa's estranged daughter was not just a doctor but a surgeon. 'I'll go and have a look anyway. Maybe she needs more help.'

He glanced at the whiteboard once more, looking for the procedure that was happening in OR Three. The letters MVA were written on the schedule.

Diego frowned. Junior surgeons shouldn't be operating on a car crash victim unsupervised. With cases like that there was no telling what might await them once they opened up the patient.

He left the nurses' station with a nod towards the nurse who had paged him and arrived at the OR just in time to see the team wrapping up the surgery.

Through the thick glass of the scrub room it was hard to read their mood. One of the junior surgeons was dressing the wound while the other one was talking to the woman he presumed was the new chief of medicine. His eyes glided over her. He appreciated the fact that he had a moment to check her out before she knew he was there.

Her hair was hidden underneath a generic grey surgical cap and her face remained behind the mask. She looked pale under the surgical lights, almost unwell, with a soft sheen of sweat covering her forehead. Was she nervous?

Diego was about to enter the OR when the new chief lifted her head and looked directly at him. Her forehead furrowed for a moment, and he felt an unexpected flash of passion uncoil itself in his chest when their gazes collided. Her golden-brown eyes widened in recognition and he knew it was her. He would have recognised those eyes anywhere.

The woman who had been stuck in his head for the last four weeks.

Ana.

Diego struggled to comprehend this revelation. For a few heartbeats they stared at each other. His thoughts were racing. Ana was Eliana Oliveira. Vanderson's sister. The second the thought manifested itself in his head the puzzle pieces fell into place and he couldn't believe he hadn't seen it the night they met.

They had the same colour hair, that dark brown shade with just a hint of red, and even without seeing the rest of her face he noticed the similarities in their eyes. This was Vanderson's sister. The woman he had spent one incredible night with.

How was this possible? They had spoken about their lives, had they not?

He tried hard to remember what they had spoken about, but the only part of that night remaining vivid in his memories were the hours they'd spent together in bed. He remembered the feel of her skin on his, his tongue trailing down her sternum, her cries of pleasure when his mouth found her essence…

The last memory made Diego shiver with renewed desire and anticipation.

How could he not have seen that she was Vanderson's sister? Now that he knew it seemed so obvious. She had even said that she'd just come from her father's funeral. Though he now knew that to be a lie. He had been at the funeral, and had kept an eye out for the unexpected heiress of the Costa fortune.

But what were they supposed to do now?

He could see the flame in her own eyes, mirroring the instant desire that flashed through him. It seemed their night together had done little to satisfy her hunger, either. Or was he reading too much into one brief glimpse?

Eliana was rooted to the spot. She blinked once to shake away the shock, and then her eyes found their way back to the surgeon standing in front of her.

From the corner of her eye she saw Diego following every movement she made. Tiny flames were igniting across her skin. For a second, the sight of him even drowned out the renewed nausea that had started up at the end of the surgery. Eliana was glad she hadn't had to operate herself after all. She could feel trembles going through her body. This wasn't just nerves, she thought. She must have caught a stomach bug.

'Make sure you page me if there are any changes in the patient's vital signs,' she said to the junior surgeon, who nodded and left as the patient was wheeled out on a gurney.

She peeled herself out of the surgical gown, pulled both gloves and mask off before removing the cap, closing her eyes for a moment and taking a few deep breaths to compose herself.

The last person she had expected to see here—
the last person she'd *wanted* to see—had just
shown up in the OR.

Diego stood in front of her, tall and hand-
somely dark. His appearance came with so
many questions Eliana didn't even know where
to start. He was a doctor. Not only that, he must
also be a surgeon if he felt comfortable coming into an operating room just like that. And,
even worse, by the looks of it he was a surgeon
at *her* hospital.

If he lived here in Rio, what had he been
doing at the hotel last month? Eliana had
thought she would never see him again.

How to start such a conversation? She didn't
even know where to begin.

She opened her mouth and immediately
closed it again as another wave of nausea
churned her stomach. Her hand flew to her
mouth, covering it on the off-chance that something might escape. Standing still, she took another deep breath to steady herself.

'Are you okay?' Diego asked, his voice
sounding distant and yet strained with concern.

Eliana tried to speak again, but she only
moved her hand away from her mouth a couple
of millimetres before feeling ill again. Keeping
her palm pressed against her lips, she shook her
head, and a second later Diego's muscular arm
wrapped itself around her waist as he guided

her towards a small stool at the far side of the operating room.

He popped up in her field of vision when he crouched down in front of her, a concerned expression on his face. The warmth she saw in his eyes would have sent her heart rate through the roof in any other circumstances, but the way she was feeling right now she was thankful to have someone there who wasn't a complete stranger.

That thought caused a slight twinge in her chest—something she couldn't focus on. Her mind was too absorbed with whatever illness it was that was making her stomach perform loops within her.

Diego's hand pressed against her forehead for a moment. 'You don't feel warm,' he said. 'But you are sweaty and, from the looks of it, nauseated. Could be a stomach bug. Did you eat anything this morning?'

Deep breaths had calmed her stomach just a bit, and Eliana dared once more to move her hand away from her mouth to answer his question. 'No, just coffee. I woke up feeling like this already, and one glance at food made my stomach turn.'

Diego frowned at her. 'You should know that coffee isn't a substitute for a proper breakfast.'

Under any other circumstances she would not have let him lecture her, but she was feeling increasingly lightheaded. The room around her darkened and turned, giving her a sense of vertigo that worsened the nausea.

'I think I'm going to pass out…' she whispered, sensing her impending doom.

She felt his hands grab her shoulders as her eyes closed. He mumbled something to her in a distorted voice, but the meaning of his words didn't reach her mind as she slipped into unconsciousness.

CHAPTER THREE

A BRIGHT LIGHT was trying its best to find a path underneath her closed eyelids. Eliana moved her head to one side to escape the glare. Her temples were throbbing, and her tongue clung to the roof of her mouth as if she hadn't had any water in days. Her lips felt dry as she opened her mouth slightly.

She heard a soft rustling above her, then hushed whispers of conversation, and it was only then that her confused mind realised that she did not know where she was. The thought penetrated the thick fog around her, and she slowly opened her eyes.

An older woman was looking at her with a friendly sparkle in her eyes. She wore a white coat and was putting on some disposable gloves. Squinting at her, Eliana read her name tag: *Dr Sophia Salvador, Accident and Emergency Services.*

'Welcome back, Chief. You gave us all quite a scare when we saw Dr Ferrari carrying your limp body.' Dr Salvador smiled at her before turning to the tray next to her. 'I'll take some blood for a test, to make sure you're okay. But your pulse ox is normal, and pupillary response is also fine. Probably thanks to Dr Ferrari, here, who cushioned your fall.'

Eliana nodded her silent consent, trying to remember what had happened as the woman drew her blood. She'd woken up this morning feeling rotten, as if she had come down with the flu. She had put it down to nerves about her new job. It wasn't the first time she had felt sick to her stomach because of nerves.

Eliana groaned as she understood what had just happened. Despite her best efforts to look as if she knew what she was doing—as if she belonged here—she had managed to faint. On her first day at work. In front of the incredibly hot almost-stranger she had met at a bar a month ago.

Memories of Diego came rushing back into her consciousness, worsening her headache as a cascade of hot sparks rampaged through her body, igniting her already frayed nerves. 'Wait…where…?'

She looked to where Dr Salvador had nodded, and winced when she tilted her head to the side too fast, causing pain to spear through her throbbing head. Diego was sitting on a chair a few paces away from the bed she lay in.

He got up when she looked at him, his expression still a lot more worried than she'd thought it would be. Snippets of what had happened in the operating room drifted back to her. He'd been holding her when she'd regained consciousness, lifting her off her seat.

Dim memories of him examining her while she was lying down on a gurney came to life in her head. Had it only been a couple of minutes ago? Her sense of time was off kilter. Had he been waiting here this entire time, watching over her?

The thought drove a different heat through her body. Not once in her life had someone watched over her. Being raised by nannies and teachers had taught her early that she was the only person in her life she could count on. Everyone else had their own agenda and she would only ever be an instrument in their achieving it.

What were his reasons for staying with her? What did Diego want? Those intrusive thoughts crawled into her head before Eliana could stop them. They had only spent one night together. There was nothing more to it.

'Let me expedite your lab results so we can release you as soon as possible,' Sophia said as she picked up the phial with her blood sample. 'From the symptoms Dr Ferrari described, and my own examination, I think a stomach bug is likely.'

The woman left, and when the door behind her fell shut silence enveloped the room for a few heartbeats as she searched for the right thing to say. It seemed it was true. Diego had not only brought her here, he'd stayed to watch over her.

She almost laughed at that thought—at how foreign and unbelievable it felt in her mind. This must be some kind of professional scheming. She was the new chief of medicine, after all.

Yet she could see a hint of concern still etched into his expression as she turned her head to look around her. She paused to look at him for a heartbeat. She opened her mouth, ready to say something, but words wouldn't form in her brain, so she looked back down to her hands, her heart suddenly pounding against her chest at the sight of the worried spark in his eyes.

It was only then that she noticed her surroundings. It was a private room, the interior much more luxurious than she had expected any hospital room to be. The sheets were soft against her skin, the mattress comfortable beneath her. The door to an en-suite bathroom stood ajar, giving her a view of the room which had a large rain shower.

'This is not the emergency department. What is this room?' she asked, forgetting about Diego's dark gaze for a second. How could this be a room in a hospital?

Diego looked around himself, and she saw an expression of contempt fluttering over his face before he regained full composure.

'This is one of the rooms Marco had designed for his various VIP patients. When I arrived with you at A&E they insisted on moving you here once they'd assessed you. They thought you had passed out from exhaustion. Do you remember?' He furrowed his brow.

'Vaguely… The whole thing is just a blur of light and headaches right now.' Eliana looked at the opulence of this place. It was fancier than her hotel room. 'This seems…excessive. I don't want to know what budgets got cut to make this happen.'

She wanted her patients to convalesce in peace and comfort, but this looked more like a room in a spa than a hospital.

Her train of thought stopped mid-track when she looked up at Diego, who had a thoughtful smile on his face as he regarded her. The gentleness in his expression sent sparks flying all over her body.

'I said the same thing when Marco started working on these rooms. Turns out he cut each department's pro bono fund to basically nothing.'

The thought seemed to fill him with renewed resentment for her father.

'You didn't get along with my father?'

As her father had hired all the department heads at the hospital, Eliana had assumed they were his minions. The people he had hired would no doubt also think it acceptable to banish a pregnant woman from the only place she had ever called home. Like Marco had done with her mother.

But it seemed she had found another person who shared her opinion about her father. How odd to think the stranger she'd had a one-night stand with four weeks ago was now her potential ally in this hospital…

Diego snorted a derisive laugh. 'Marco Costa would have fired me ages ago if he could, and over the years I gave him enough reasons to try. But he only ever caught me with my little toe over the line and nothing else,' he said, and shrugged. 'By the time he realised I would be more trouble than my talent was worth it was already too late. If he'd let me go half of his staff would have walked out with me.'

He said it so matter-of-factly Eliana had no choice but to admire his confidence. It took a lot to know one's worth. But there was something else hidden in his words, too. A sense of accountability and belonging. And from those words alone she knew exactly who Diego considered his people.

It was a thought that made envy needle at her heart. Belonging was a foreign concept to

Eliana. She'd grown up isolated from the only family she had ever known—which hadn't been much to begin with—and her experience at boarding school had been little better.

'Sorry, I know he was your father—' he started, but she interrupted him with a shake of her head.

'You might remember me saying how I wasn't close to my father back at that hotel bar. Your words are docile compared to what I have to say about him on any given day.'

Understanding rushed over his expression, but it only remained there for a moment before his face slackened again. He was clearly not letting her see his thoughts.

But he must know about her. Everyone in this hospital did. In the thirty-five years since her birth—since her mother had fallen for a guy she never should have—the staff of Santa Valeria had not forgotten the scandal surrounding her conception. From the moment Eliana had set foot in the foyer of the hospital she'd been able to sense the eyes on her, the whispers following her around as she was introduced to different staff members.

Even Diego, who of course hadn't worked here when her mother had got pregnant, must know about her—how she had grown up as the black sheep of the Costa family, escaping her abusive home the moment she'd turned eighteen.

'I'm sorry,' he said, and somehow she knew they both understood in that moment what he was apologising for. Not for something that he'd done, but for the circumstances that had led to him knowing so much about her.

'So, you think Santa Valeria should do more pro bono surgeries?' Eliana asked, going back to what he had said about the budget cut.

'Among other things, yes,' he said, crossing his arms in front of his chest and giving her a view she didn't want to dwell on. She knew the strength those arms possessed. She had found pleasure in them throughout their entire night together.

'What else do you suggest?'

It was a genuine question for the man she'd thought she would never meet again, only to find out that they would now be working together—at least until she went back home in a couple of weeks.

Diego tilted his head to one side, his eyes narrowing as he looked at her with such intensity that her breath caught in her throat. His hand wandered up to his face, stroking over the light stubble covering his cheeks.

'Community outreach. We have some high-calibre donors supporting us. Instead of building private suites and taking those donors on lavish cruises, we could take Santa Valeria's facilities and help the poorer communities in this city when they are most in need of care. God knows there are enough people requiring help right now.'

His words seemed to her to come from a place of experience, with a small nugget of truth shining through.

'Why is that important to you?' she asked, and almost flinched when his eyes grew darker, narrowing on her. Her question seemed to have crossed an invisible boundary.

His jaw tightened for a moment as he stared her down, but Eliana forced herself to meet his gaze straight on, despite the defences she spotted going up all around him.

'It's the right thing to do. I might have got out, but they are still my people.'

'Your—?'

The door opened, interrupting their conversation, and Dr Salvador strode back into the room. The fierce protectiveness in Diego's eyes vanished, leaving his face unreadable.

Eliana's eyes were drawn to the emergency doctor, who stepped closer. She was wearing an expression of medical professionalism on her face that quickened her pulse. She knew that look. She had given it to patients herself.

She whipped her head around, looking at Diego, and whatever he saw written in her face was enough to make him get off his chair and step closer to her side. A similar look of protectiveness to the one he'd had a few moments ago was etched into his features.

'Would you mind giving us some privacy?' Sophia asked him, and a tremble shook Eliana's body.

The nausea came rushing back, her head suddenly felt light, and Eliana reacted before she could think, her hand reaching for Diego's and crushing it in a vice-like grip.

'It's okay if he stays,' she said, in a voice that sounded so unlike her own.

Something deep within her told her she needed him to stay. Whether it was premonition or just a primal fear gripping at her heart, she didn't know.

Diego stopped, giving her a questioning look, but he stayed, and his hand did not fight her touch.

'Well, it looks like it's not a stomach bug, but morning sickness. Or, in your case, late-afternoon sickness.' She paused for a moment, before confirming the absurd thought that was rattling around in Eliana's head. 'You're pregnant.'

Eliana opened her mouth to speak, but no words crossed the threshold of her lips. Pregnant? How was she pregnant? Her head snapped around to Diego, and whatever expression she was wearing on her face seemed to convey to him all the words she didn't want to say in front of the doctor.

The baby was his. *They* were pregnant.

His hand slipped from her grasp as he took a step back. The shock she felt at the revelation was written on his face.

'How long?' she asked, even though she knew it didn't matter.

Eliana had only slept with one person in the last six months, and that was the man standing here in the room with her.

'I can't say without an ultrasound. Do you remember the date of your last period?' Dr Salvador paused for a moment, to give her time to digest the information, before she continued, 'Normally I would get someone from OBGYN down here to talk to you, but since this is your hospital, and you're a doctor yourself, I'll discharge you. But make sure you start your prenatal care straight away.'

Her last period? She had no idea. Her periods were always irregular and hard to track—something she'd made peace with a long time ago. When she didn't have one, she didn't believe anything amiss.

Four weeks. That was when she'd fallen pregnant. Because that was when she had met Diego.

Eliana didn't register Dr Salvador's words, her mind too busy trying to understand the new and unexpected reality she found herself in. As if her life hadn't been complicated enough, with her father's death. Now she could add an unplanned pregnancy to the pile.

A baby growing right below her heart.

Her hand darted to her still flat stomach.

'All right, I'll leave you to digest this information. But medically you're good to go about your day.'

Sophia Salvador left them, closing the door behind her.

Every muscle in his body was tense with anticipation in a strange fight-or-flight response to the situation. His mind was reeling from the explosive information Sophia had just shared with them, and he was struggling to make any sense of it.

He'd had about a million questions floating around in his mind, but he didn't know how to verbalise any of them now he'd heard her say those words, acknowledging out loud what Eliana's eyes had already told him. How was he supposed to start this conversation?

Diego grabbed a chair from the far side of the room and brought it closer to the bed, sitting down and looking at her. 'Am I—?'

Eliana nodded before he'd finished his sentence. 'It's yours. There's no doubt about it. I've not slept with anyone else.'

There it was.

A large boulder dropped into his stomach as she said those words. Their one night of searing passion had resulted in a child.

'That's not what I expected to hear when I saw you again today,' was all he managed to say, his mind going blank. All he could think of was that life-altering revelation.

Eliana gave a short laugh, and Diego wasn't sure whether it was genuine. He barely knew the woman lying on the bed in front of him. It was a thought that made him laugh in return. The mother of his child was nothing more than a stranger to him.

'I don't even know how it happened,' she said in a quiet voice, more as if she was talking to herself than to him. 'I'm on the pill…'

Her voice trailed off, and there was a thoughtful expression on her face. Then her eyes went wide with shock and her hand darted up to her mouth, clasping it with a gasp.

Diego stiffened in his chair, reaching out to her. 'What is it?'

'It's my fault. When I came here last month it was after the news of my father and brother's accident. I was nervous and felt ill. I went through my morning routine, including taking the pill, and then…' She stopped and looked at him. 'I threw up. I threw up the medication. But I didn't even think about it because I didn't think I was going to meet someone.'

That explained it. On the night in question they'd had that conversation every responsible adult should have about avoiding unwanted consequences of their consensual encounter. Diego had even worn a condom that first time. Maybe even the second time.

His memories became blurry around the third time, with the night growing longer and the passion hotter, each union burning more intensely than the one before. Her touch had been intoxicating—to the point where he could remember little else about that night.

He couldn't say it was her fault. It might just as well be his. *Theirs.* But the fact was they were now bound to each other through the life they'd created.

'It's not anyone's fault. These things happen—you know that as well as I do.'

He knew that wasn't reassuring, but in this moment—with the shock of discovery still sitting deep in his bones—he didn't know what else to tell her. Or how to ask the question burning on his lips. This was her choice, after all.

Whether it was his expression or the unexpected connection they suddenly shared he didn't know, but Eliana seemed to have read his thoughts, for a moment later she said, 'I don't have a plan, but I'm not abandoning this child the way I was disregarded. The rest I can figure out.'

Something strange bubbled up within his chest at her words. A feeling of heavy responsibility, but with something lurking underneath it as well. A protectiveness unlike anything he had experienced before.

'The rest *we* can figure out,' he said.

Her eyes narrowed as she looked at him. 'Are you up to the task of being a father?' she asked rather bluntly, zeroing in on a vulnerability that he hadn't shared with her yet.

His mind had always struggled to comprehend the enormity of what fatherhood meant. His father had been such an abject failure in teaching him what it meant to be a decent person. Instead of raising him, Ignacio Ferrari had given the young Diego to his mother—*avozinha*—to raise while he went sleeping around all of Rio.

How could he be a proud Latin father in a world where the odds had been stacked against him from the very beginning and his own father had been the worst possible role model? There were things he would have to teach his child, weren't there?

'That's going to be one of those things we'll have to figure out,' he said with a wry smile.

He rested his face in his hands for a moment, pressing his fingers against his temples in a reminder to himself to stay collected. The tension was gone, but it had been replaced by a reality they were both starting to understand.

'Diego, this is a lot to consider. I need some time to think about your…' Eliana didn't finish her sentence, prompting him to raise an eyebrow at her.

Diego straightened his back to look at her. 'My what? This is my child, too. Whatever you may have heard about me from gossiping staff, I don't shy away from my responsibilities.'

He'd made up his mind. For better or for worse, they were in it for the long run. He didn't know how to be a father, but at least he knew how to be around children. His father had created so many offspring, all of them sooner or later arriving at his grandmother's house to get to know their family, that he had experience with all the different stages of childhood.

'What do you want us to do?' he asked, and watched as she shook her head.

'I don't know, Diego. Right now, I can't handle any thought of *us* in this context. I came here to find someone to lead this hospital—not *this*.'

The silence between them grew tense as he watched different emotions flutter over her face, as if she was chasing her own thoughts in her head. He reached his hand out to her—only to stop when a soft buzzing interrupted him.

Diego frowned as he checked his phone. 'They're paging me for a Code Blue. I have to go.'

Eliana nodded, her face blank except for her golden-brown eyes, which were still wide in shock.

'Can we talk about this later?' He didn't want to leave. He wanted to stay and for them to work through this life-altering news together. Especially when she was still so fragile from earlier.

'Go and attend to your patient. I need some time to think. I…' She hesitated for a moment, finally looking at him, and he could see the doubt swirling in her eyes. 'I need some space to work through this. I'll let you know when I'm ready to talk.'

His phone kept on vibrating, and Diego hissed a low curse as he turned around to rush to his patient, his mind still reeling at the way his life had changed for ever in the last two hours.

He was going to be a father.

CHAPTER FOUR

ELIANA SPENT THE better part of two weeks looking for her replacement. The news about her unexpected pregnancy still sat deep in her bones, and she had yet to make a plan. Or talk to Diego about it. Staying locked up in her office interviewing people had made it easy to avoid him, as she didn't know what to tell him. Planning had never been her strength.

'Everything else we can figure out.'

That was what Diego had said. As if they were a team now. Fused together by their one night of passion.

She would have to make a plan with him. Whether or not she wanted Diego in her life didn't matter any more. Eliana had grown up deprived of both parents, so if Diego was willing to be a father she would make sure he could be a part of their child's life. Regardless of how she felt about him.

'Good morning, Suelen,' Eliana said as she passed the desk of her assistant and waited for her to hand her the usual diary full of appointments and a list of important queries she had to attend to as the interim chief of medicine.

But her assistant had only one item on her agenda. 'You asked me to schedule you some time in the emergency department today. Dr Salvador is expecting you.'

'That's right. I almost forgot about that.' She'd asked Suelen to block off some time with each department head so she could observe different procedures. Diego had already alluded to the changes he would like to see at Santa Valeria, and he wasn't the only department head with a wish list.

Even though Eliana yearned for some OR time, her first stop had to be the emergency department under Sophia Salvador. It was the beating heart of their entire trauma centre, and deserved a lot more attention than it seemed it had previously received.

Eliana went inside her office to put down her jacket and bag, and then came out and stopped in front of her assistant's desk again, when a thought dawned on her. There was something she needed to do and had been avoiding for the last couple of days.

'Can you get the obstetrics head up here for a meeting as soon as they have time? I have some matters to discuss.'

Those 'matters' being her child.

She balled her hand into a fist to stop herself from reaching for her stomach. That instinctual protectiveness emerged every time she thought of the tiny being inside her, but she wasn't ready to reveal anything to the world just yet.

Eliana was aware of the looks and whispers following her around, reviving the rumours around her mother's affair with the old chief. Who knew how the conversations would turn when they found out that she was in a similar position—pregnant with the baby of a high-ranking doctor in this hospital? She was still a stranger to everyone here, and didn't dare risk showing any kind of vulnerability. Things had got so bad for her own mother she'd ended up fleeing this place.

An old pain clawed at her heart, and not for the first time she wished her mother were still alive to give her some advice. Had she ever regretted what had happened with her father? Would Diego turn out to be a similar man?

One day at a time, she told herself as she walked to the emergency department. Only time would tell what kind of parents she and Diego would be together.

The second Eliana stepped through the doors to A&E noise erupted around her as nurses and doctors saw to their patients, with ailments of varying degrees of seriousness. She tried her best not to stand in anyone's way as she walked to the far end of the room, looking at a large screen on the wall that held all the information on their current intakes.

'Who are you?' the nurse behind the counter asked her, tearing her gaze away from the screen.

'I'm—'

She was interrupted by Sophia walking into sight. 'Chief Oliveira, I was wondering when you would show up. Our admissions board is already full, so you won't mind getting to work straight away?'

'Work?' Eliana raised her eyebrows.

When she'd scheduled this time she hadn't expected any of the department heads to put her to work. Though she was quite excited at the idea of practising medicine. Being the chief of medicine involved a lot more paperwork than patients—a fact she lamented.

'You wanted to get to know my department. There is no better way than to work here for a day—and we can always use a hand.' Sophia turned around and looked over at the screen. 'Why don't you look at Bed Four? One of our regulars is back, and she'll have lots to say about her time at your hospital.'

'All right.'

Eliana smiled, liking this idea more by the minute. She'd thought she would have to wait until she was back in Belo Horizonte to see patients again. This was an exciting change of pace from her usual chief's duties.

Stepping up to Bed Four, Eliana grabbed the patient chart attached to the end of the bed and scanned it. The intake nurse had scribbled *'shortness of breath and palpitations'* on the form, at which Eliana raised an eyebrow. Why had they left a patient with these symptoms unattended?

The older woman was lying down, giving the impression of sleeping at first glance, but she was actually reading a somewhat tattered-looking book as she lay on her side. Her chest was heaving with laboured breaths, but other than that she seemed unperturbed by her struggle to breathe.

'*Olá, senhora*, I'm Dr Oliveira. Do you mind if I have a listen to your breathing?'

The woman turned her head as if she had only just noticed her. 'I haven't seen you around. Are you new?'

Not a question she had expected. 'That I am,' she answered after a short silence. 'And Dr Salvador has already told me this isn't your first visit.'

Eliana looked at the chart again, but the only part filled out on the admission form was the first name: Selma.

'I'm here more often than I would like, and it takes me a whole day to get here. I usually go to the clinic close to home, but the doctor hasn't been there in a while.' An expression of concern fluttered over her face. 'He said I should come here whenever I need help managing my condition.'

'Condition?' Eliana arched her brows.

Selma put her book down on her lap and grabbed her bag, digging through it to produce a small notebook with torn edges and crinkled paper. She licked her finger to help her turn the pages as she searched for the right one.

'He's such a helpful and kind man, so he wrote it down for me…along with everything the other doctors will need to know. It's called…' She paused, squinting at the words scrawled on the paper. 'Pulmonary hyper…'

'Hypertension?' Eliana asked when Selma struggled with reading the next word. 'Can I see the doctor's notes?'

Someone with such a serious condition should be under the continuous care of a physician. Why had this doctor told her to come to *this* hospital?

If the clinic is closed, go to the Santa Valeria General Hospital. If they refuse to treat you, ask to page Dr V. Costa.

Eliana's heart stuttered in her chest when she read the words written on the piece of paper.

She stared at the ink in disbelief. Her *brother* had told this woman to come here.

Selma had said the doctor hadn't been at the clinic for a while. Was Vanderson the physician in question? Her eyes went back to the woman, scrutinising her. She clearly didn't know about his death.

'Have you stopped taking your medication?'

Among the scribbles describing Selma's condition, she could see that she had been prescribed benazepril, a type of medication to treat high blood pressure in older patients.

'Well, yes, I go by the clinic to get my medication from the doctor. But since he hasn't been there for a while I had no choice but to stop.'

'You don't have a GP who can fill your prescription for you?'

Eliana was confident she knew the answer to that question, but she wanted to ask anyway.

They could only be one reason why her brother had instructed this woman to come to his father's hospital's emergency department. Because she had nowhere else to go and she needed to be treated.

Selma's expression faltered for a brief moment. She glanced around, as if uncertain what to say.

Noticing the hesitation, Eliana quickly shook her head. 'Never mind about that. There's probably some built-up fluid in your lungs. We'll treat you for that, and I will stock up your supply of medication. No questions asked.'

She smiled to reassure the patient, before moving away to get a portable ultrasound machine as well as a set of hypodermic needles and syringes to drain the excess fluid compressing Selma's lungs.

Still new to the hospital—and to the emergency department in particular—it took her a couple of minutes to find the right closet and the materials necessary to do the procedure.

The newfound knowledge about the steps her brother had taken to help this patient had unleashed a torrent of different emotions in her chest, mingling with the still-fresh news of her unexpected pregnancy. It was becoming harder for her to focus on just one thing when every day came with a new revelation about herself, her family, or the hospital she now owned.

The thoughts swirling in her head came to an abrupt halt when she spotted someone next to Selma's bed. Diego stood beside the woman, holding his stethoscope to her chest as he examined her.

Eliana froze in place, her senses overwhelmed by Diego's sudden appearance. Her flight reaction kicked in, urging her to turn around and run—as she had been doing for the last two weeks whenever she saw him. But this time her feet didn't heed the command, staying rooted to the spot as an instant and visceral awareness of him thundered through her. The new information about her brother was forgotten as longing gripped her, unexpected in its intensity.

They hadn't spoken since they'd received the news about her unexpected pregnancy, and Eliana knew that was her doing. Diego had tried to reach out, asking for time to talk. Time she had yet to grant him. Because she didn't know what he was going to say as much as she didn't know what *she* would say.

After all, making plans had always been her greatest weakness. And the decisions they were supposed to make together required a lot of co-ordination and planning.

Eliana forced herself to take a deep breath, shaking away the shock of seeing him. There was still a patient who needed her help, and she couldn't get distracted by her personal issues.

She stepped up to the bed, clearing her throat to gain their attention. 'I didn't expect to see you here, Dr Ferrari,' she said as she passed him.

'I can say the same thing about you, Chief,' he replied, and Eliana could swear she heard a hint of reproach in his voice.

Sparks filled the air the second they were close enough to touch, igniting a longing heat just behind her belly button. It was a reaction completely inappropriate, and so out of control it almost made her flinch. The second he came too close to her all her inhibitions seemed to melt away, and she just wanted to be a part of him again.

With his own wing being as busy as it was, Diego didn't have the freedom to answer pages that weren't work-related as fast as he would like to. So when the admissions nurse in the emergency department had paged him about a patient from the free clinic it had taken him almost an hour to get there and check for himself.

What he hadn't expected was to see Eliana taking care of his patient.

A thrill of excitement mixed with dread in his stomach. While the need to see her pulled at his chest, he didn't want to do it in front of Selma, because he might have to explain some things he didn't know how to.

The new chief didn't know about the free clinic he was running—sometimes using hospital resources like medicine, or time from him and his colleagues. Everyone he'd ever involved in helping out had done so voluntarily, and with the understanding that they might be in a grey zone where the hospital policies were concerned. They were helping people who needed assistance—even if Diego had to beg, borrow and steal from Santa Valeria.

What he hadn't decided was if he wanted to tell Eliana about his side project or if he should lie low until a new chief was appointed and deal with them.

Oblivious to the tension zipping like electricity between them, Selma beamed at Eliana. 'You didn't mention that you knew Dr Ferrari. Does that mean we'll see *you* at the clinic as well?'

A boulder dropped into Diego's stomach. So much for finding his own way of broaching the subject with Eliana.

'I was paged here for a consult when I saw you, Selma,' he lied, and in an almost automated gesture he took the instruments Eliana was carrying into his own hands to start the procedure.

'Do you tend to take a lot of the consultations registrars should be doing?' she asked.

Her voice had an edge to it, but not one of hostility. Was she amused by his attempt to cover up the true reason he was down here? What had Selma already told her?

Unwilling to drop the charade, Diego shrugged. 'They're better off studying procedures in the OR rather than looking at every sprained ankle that comes into this place.' He paused for a moment and couldn't help but flash a grin at Eliana. 'I'm that good.'

The surprise his shameless innuendo brought to her face caused the heat of desire to flash through his body. He knew better than to indulge those feelings by flirting with her, no matter how subtly. But whenever he got close enough to her, control slipped through his fingers and he was seduced into forgetting why he couldn't be with anyone. *Ever*.

Especially not the woman carrying his child.

It had been two weeks since the news broke, and yet those two words together still sounded strange in his ears. *His child*. Diego was going to be a father when he didn't know the first thing about doing it.

He would never be with someone just for the sake of a child. Diego would be there for his kid—sure. But that was as much as he could give.

Eliana was now ignoring his flirtatious attempts at conversation and was focusing on the patient instead. 'Your pulmonary hypertension has caused fluid to build up in what's called the pleural space. May I move your gown down a bit to access your chest?'

Selma nodded and sat up, pushing her feet past the edge of the bed, while Eliana wheeled a small tray table around for the patient to lean on so she would have access to her back. Diego had already performed a thoracentesis on her, with the help of a cardiologist. The thorax wasn't an anatomical space he was familiar with, but in his efforts to providing healthcare to the disadvantaged people of the city he'd had to learn a lot of procedures that lay outside his expertise.

'To drain the fluid we'll use a needle to get to the space between your lungs and your chest wall. That should allow you to breathe easier. This will be cold for a bit.'

She dabbed some cool gel onto the patient's skin and then surprised Diego when she handed him the transducer.

'I will do the procedure—you can assist,' she said, in a voice that didn't leave any room for negotiation, which made it that much harder for him not to argue.

'I'm familiar with the steps of a thoracentesis,' he said, and watched as her eyes narrowed on him, the golden sparks losing their warm light right in front of him.

'Is it a common procedure in your orthopaedic cases?'

Diego had seen the trap he'd laid for himself before she had even opened her mouth, and he cursed himself silently. Some primal force in his chest had urged him to prove himself to her in any way possible. Show her that he could provide for her and their child. Look after them the way his father had never looked after him.

The blood froze in his veins as the jumble of thoughts caught up with him, rendering him mute for a couple of heartbeats. Where had *that* come from? Their night together had altered his life for ever, but that didn't mean they were meant to be anything more than co-parents.

'You know it's not,' he answered in a low growl when he found his voice again. The unexpected depth and chaos of his feelings towards Eliana had thrown him so much he had to remind himself where he was.

'Then you can take the ultrasound while I perform the thoracentesis.'

Eliana prepared the needle and syringe while he sat down on a small stool next to the bed. He made eye contact with Selma as he placed the transducer on her sternum to show Eliana what she needed to see.

'The pressure will be uncomfortable. I'm sorry. I'll try to be as fast as possible,' she said as she looked at the screen of the ultrasound machine for a moment, surveying the field.

Diego watched Eliana's hands as they probed the patient's ribs for a moment before she picked up the needle with her right hand and inserted it in the ninth intercostal space—quick, but precise—her eyes only occasionally leaving the ultrasound screen to look at Selma over her shoulder.

'You're doing great. I've positioned the needle, so we can begin the drain.'

Even though Selma was staring ahead, Eliana kept a gentle and reassuring smile on her face, making him wonder about the work she had been doing before she came to Santa Valeria. The way she'd handled the patient so far was unlike anything he'd ever seen from Marco. He would never have spent his time in any department helping out. He'd valued his own time above patient care.

Diego was relieved to see this wasn't the case for his daughter. Eliana clearly knew how to explain every step of the procedure so her patient knew throughout what was happening. After Marco Costa and his 'money first' attitude towards healthcare, she was exactly the kind of chief of medicine Santa Valeria needed.

Selma winced, and Diego grabbed her hand with his free one, keeping the other steady so that Eliana could do her work.

'Remember to take slow breaths, just like last time. Once we're done, you can rest, and I'll ask the nurse to bring you some books from the library.'

He knew Selma well. Her high blood pressure needed to be controlled with medication, but without medical insurance she could only ever get help from the emergency department when things got as bad as they were now.

'I'll be fine. I need to get back home and pick up my grandson before my daughter has to go to work, so I can't stay too long.'

Diego saw a frown appear on Eliana's face as she listened to their conversation, and he could almost hear the thoughts in her head. She'd want Selma to stay for observation—a wish he shared. But he knew that Selma had no option to stay. Her daughter's work was keeping all of them fed.

He had seen the same thing in his grandmother as well. She had worked herself to the bone to help her grandchildren achieve a better life, to escape the *favelas*, and Diego counted himself fortunate in being able to repay her for her efforts. She had been the only consistent parental figure in his life, raising him after his father had dumped him at her house when he had been busy cheating on his mother. Only to retrieve him again once his parents had 'fixed' their marriage and wanted to pretend they were a family again.

'And we are done,' Eliana said after a couple more minutes had passed, and put her instruments down. She pulled the gloves off her hands. 'I'll ask a nurse to give you the medication as well. Please get as much rest as you can and come back before you run out of medicine.'

She took the notebook that was lying on Selma's lap and stuck her hand in her pocket, retrieving a pen from it. Diego stood up from his seat, leaning to look over her shoulder. The handwriting on the page was his friend's—instructions he had written down when Selma had first sought him out for help.

He watched as Eliana struck out Vanderson's name and wrote a note beneath it, before handing it back to the patient.

'Tell them I have authorised all your treatments already, so they can give you your new medication along with a physical, okay?'

Selma nodded, and a moment later Diego felt Eliana's deep brown eyes were on him, peering so deeply he thought she was staring straight inside him, past all the locked barriers he had put up.

But she didn't say anything. Instead, she turned around on her heel and hurried off.

'Ana, esperar!' This was the first time they had spoken to each other since the bombshell announcement of her pregnancy. 'Where are you going?'

He caught up to her in three big strides, taking her by the elbow and leading her into a free exam room at the far end of the emergency department. Closing the door behind him, he flipped the lock so they wouldn't be interrupted.

Hot sparks travelled up and down her arm where Diego had just touched her. Despite his insistence, his fingers had been gentle as he'd guided her to this empty room so they could talk.

A talk Eliana knew had been coming—and yet she didn't feel the least bit prepared. They needed to talk about their child and what their lives would look like as co-parents. The strong surges of desire infusing the fibres of her body didn't help in untangling the mess she found herself in.

She couldn't trust her feelings. Not when everything was so foggy and tangled up.

Diego stood in front of her, his corded arms crossed in front of his impressive chest as he heaved a long sigh. The lines around his eyes told her he had been struggling just as much as she had in the last two weeks. Was he struggling to cope? Or was he trying to find the best way out of the situation?

A sudden fear gripped at her chest when she thought about him running away. Would he really do that?

'What are you doing down here? Shouldn't you be…?' His voice trailed off.

'Shouldn't I be what? Resting?' Eliana scoffed, hoping he had stopped himself from completing his sentence because he'd realised how ridiculous he sounded. Though the protectiveness in his voice had kicked something loose within her that made her heart stutter in her chest.

He was worried about her.

'I'm sorry. I know I'm not handling this situation very well.'

He looked at her, and the spark in his dark brown eyes was so disarming that her breath caught in her throat. She thought she could forgive him anything as long as he promised to look at her like that for ever.

Eliana hesitated for a moment before extending an olive branch. 'I've scheduled some time with each of the department heads so I can get to know their service. The emergency department seemed a good place to start, since I spend a lot of time there at my own hospital.'

Diego dropped his arms to his sides as he relaxed a bit. 'Where is your hospital?'

'In Belo Horizonte. I did my training there, and they asked me to stay on after I got my general surgeon certification. I took a short break between my certification and starting my new role and then…well, you know what happened.'

Diego nodded.

A frown was pulling on his lips and it made her chest contract. She wanted to reach out and smooth the corners of his mouth up into the self-assured smile she preferred. He looked genuinely sad, which didn't match the conversation they'd had on her first day. Back then he had complained about how her father had cut spending on pro bono surgeries to build lavish rooms for his VIP patients. Why did he now seem sad at the mention of his death? Or was something else troubling him?

Her hand went to her stomach in what now felt like an automated gesture. Even though there was hardly anything to see or feel at the moment, the presence of her child comforted her more than anything else had in the last couple of weeks. Their bond was already forming, giving her strength for the challenges ahead of her.

'I want to go back to Belo Horizonte. With him. Or her. Which might make things a bit harder if you're planning on being around.'

'If?'

Something in his face contorted—a look of pain she hadn't expected. Her doubt had hurt his feelings, and she struggled to understand that for a moment. They were still hardly more than strangers who were finding themselves in a position where they had to raise a child together.

He seemed genuine in his intentions, really wanting to do what was right. It had been him, after all, chasing her around the hospital to talk about their child while she'd been avoiding him. Would he have done that if he meant to be an absentee father?

'We've never spoken about it, so I wasn't sure how you feel about your involvement,' she said, and felt his answer coming even before he spoke.

'We haven't spoken because every time I tried to approach you, you ran for the hills as if I had some contagious disease,' he retorted, with an edge of bitterness in his voice.

She deserved that, yet it still made her flinch. She hadn't been thinking about his feelings. The news had sent her into preservation mode for several days as she'd gathered her thoughts.

Because there was more than just the matter of their child to discuss. There was the attraction humming in her blood, flooding her with a sharp awareness every time she so much as glimpsed Diego somewhere in the hospital. It stood in stark contrast to her rational side, which wanted to retreat far away from this way too sexy man and let their lawyers do all the talking.

She wondered what it had been like for her mother to fall pregnant by a man she wasn't in a serious relationship with. If she had lived would she be urging Eliana to find a way to be together, even if it was just for their child?

No, her mother had been stronger than that—even if she hadn't been able to hang on to life at the end. She would have wanted her to forge her own path. It might intersect with Diego's—and she found that she really wanted him to remain in her life in one form or another—but they didn't need to be in a romantic relationship to be good parents. Even though the look he was giving her in this moment was ratcheting up a tightness in her core that she had to will away with a few breaths.

'I'm sorry.' She cast her eyes down, her hands

crossed over her still flat stomach. 'I needed some space to think, to figure out what I want to do. I think it's great that you want to be involved. In fact, I was hoping you would.'

Eliana sighed. Her limbs felt heavy all of a sudden as the day caught up to her. Selma's procedure had taken a lot more energy out of her than she had expected.

Diego must have seen her falter, for he stepped up to her, wrapping his hand around her arm. With ease, as if he was picking up a child, he grabbed her hips with his other arm and placed her on the exam room table. Her feet dangled above the floor, grazing along his thighs every now and then, and each contact created a trail of sparks that went shooting across her skin.

The attraction between them was palpable, and the glances they exchanged were heated with desire but underpinned by the gravity of their situation.

'Are you ready to talk now?' he asked her.

Regret tied a knot in her stomach when he took a step back. Even though it had been only a slight brush of her feet against his legs, she didn't want it to stop.

'I still don't have a plan. But, yes, I'm ready to talk about things.'

Only she didn't know what. If it wasn't about her plans for their child, what was there left to talk about? The way every time she closed her eyes she could smell the scent of earth and petrichor as his tongue and teeth had grazed over her neck?

'Have you already had your first prenatal appointment?'

She blinked, finding her way out of the unbidden fantasy. 'I'm actually going to speak to someone today. I asked Suelen to tell them to come see me.'

Diego's lips curled upwards in a grin that made her heart stop for a second before it continued beating twice as fast.

'Two weeks on the job and you're already making people come to you. That's a boss move, Dr Oliveira.'

She laughed, feeling some of the tension draining out of her. 'I had to learn to stand up for myself early on. That habit dies hard, no matter what job I'm in.'

'I know what you mean.'

Eliana looked at him, her head tilted to one side in a gesture of curiosity. She wanted him to elaborate but he remained silent, his face not revealing the thoughts in his mind.

'Do you want to come to the scan in a couple of weeks?' she asked.

This time his expression shifted, and she could see the beginnings of panic bubbling up in the corners of his eyes. A sentiment she understood well. Appointments, scans…those things rooted their surprise baby in reality when they were still coming to terms with the change in their lives.

Her mother had been forced to do it all by herself. Marco hadn't wanted anything to do with his affair or their child. But Diego was already showing himself to be different, wanting to be a part of the whole journey. The thought of going it alone sent terror thrumming through her body, and she wanted to trust him—trust that he would support her throughout the journey. That she could let him be a part of it without her attraction to him burning her alive.

'Yes, I would like that.'

He lifted his hands, and for a second she thought he was going to reach out to her—a thought that thundered excitement and terror through her in equal measures. But he quickly dropped them back to his sides again.

Whatever it was floating between them was affecting him too.

Their one night together had already given her all the comfort she'd get from him. Anything beyond that was never going to happen. A baby didn't change the fact that she didn't want to pursue a relationship—especially not in Rio de Janeiro, when she already had one foot out of the city.

In fact the baby just reaffirmed her feelings

about a relationship. Staying together for the sake of a child would only ever ensure that everyone involved grew resentful of one another. That kind of thing never worked out.

'When are you going back to Belo Horizonte?' he asked.

She tried to read his expression, but shutters had fallen over his eyes, revoking the access he had very briefly granted her.

'I don't know. Not for a month or two, it seems. It depends on how fast my father's estate can be wrapped up and how much work needs to be done here. This place is so different from the hospital in Belo Horizonte.'

Diego raised an eyebrow in question. 'How come?'

'Well, for starters the hospital there is part-owned by the local municipality, so the area we service is a lot more diverse than here. Though from our encounter some moments ago I can see you're trying to change that.'

Diego had the decency to look away as her words sank in. It had been obvious Selma knew him, and she had connected him to the free clinic she had mentioned during their initial chat.

'You held yourself well with her. I was glad to see the compassion in your treatment,' he said after a few moments, his lips curving in a small smile that sent her heart rate racing.

'Sounds like you didn't expect me to be a competent doctor,' she replied, willing the heat rising to her cheeks to go away.

'Not at all. I just liked seeing that we're now being led by someone who thinks of the patients first.' He stopped talking for a second. Then, 'I meant to pay you a compliment. I enjoyed watching you work.'

'Oh…' The heat within her flared out from her cheeks in every direction through her body, making it impossible for her to find the right words to reply.

Silence fell over them and grew more tense with each moment passing as neither of them spoke, each chasing their own thoughts. Eliana was bursting to say something—to set boundaries from the very beginning so things wouldn't get messy. But she didn't know how to start that conversation. Especially not if he was paying her compliments like that.

'I think we should be friends,' Diego said, throwing her completely off track with those six simple words. 'We both went into this thinking it would be a one-night stand. Neither of us wanted more than that. And I don't think either of us wants to get into a relationship just because there's a child. But if we're doing this together, we should be…friends.'

'Friends?' she repeated, as if she hadn't heard right. When she'd been thinking about boundaries, that hadn't been the approach she had thought about.

'Yes. Friends. We're going to be in each other's lives from now on, for better or for worse. Don't you think we should find a way we can be comfortable with each other without…?'

He let the pause speak for itself, but Eliana wasn't sure she understood what he meant. Without sleeping with each other again? Without acting on the intense attraction that wrapped itself around them every time they spoke?

'So, we're going from giving each other multiple orgasms as complete strangers who will never see each other again to being…friends?'

Diego cracked a smile at that, a soft chuckle escaping his gorgeous throat. 'Well, if you put it that way you make it sound like a terrible idea.'

'No, friends sounds good. I only ever had emotionally unavailable parents, so I imagine parents who are friends will be a big step up.'

Friends sounds good.

Doubt crept into her heart the second she said those words, and she fought hard not to let it be visible on her face. At several points during their conversation she had imagined running her mouth along his collarbones. Her desire for Diego was overpowering, firing a heat through her system that left the nerve-ends singed.

How was she supposed to be *friends* with

someone who stoked a fire of passion in her with mere glances?

But he was right. They were going to be in each other's lives one way or another.

Was that what her mother had been hoping for when she'd found out that she was pregnant? That she and Marco would find a way to co-exist? Would she still be alive today if Marco had made the same suggestion Diego had?

It was worth a try. She wanted her child to grow up knowing both of its parents' love and support. If that meant she needed to get over her attraction to Diego, she could do that. Right?

'So…how do we go from this…' she raised her hands, motioning around her '…to being friends?'

'Let's start by doing some activities that don't involve a sick patient. Or taking our clothes off. Something like lunch on a Saturday.'

He paused for a moment, the mischievous gleam in his eyes telling her that taking her clothes off was all he was thinking about.

Eliana took the pen out of her pocket again and pretended to take notes on her palm. 'No patients. No taking off clothes. Got it.' She paused for a moment, seemingly inspecting her invisible list. 'Can we talk about work, though? I have some questions about Selma.'

Diego let out a sigh, raking his hands through

his already unruly hair. 'I hoped you'd forget about that.'

The discussion about their child *had* made her forget for a moment. When they'd come in here she had planned on confronting him about the clinic, but their attention had quickly turned to other matters between them.

'Did you know my brother? Was he working at a free clinic somewhere in the city? Selma's notes—'

Diego raised his hands, interrupting her. 'Lunch on Saturday. I'll pick you up from your hotel. We can get to know each other. As friends.'

Eliana hesitated, suddenly not sure if meeting Diego outside of work was such a good idea. While they might both be sincere about being friends, their attraction was undeniable—and she could read it in his eyes as well. How were they supposed to dial this kind of visceral intensity back to friendship?

No matter how. They had to do it. Somehow Eliana had to learn to be around him without dissolving into a puddle of need and longing.

CHAPTER FIVE

THE COOL AIR circulating through the hotel lobby did precious little to calm Diego's nerves as he sat in one of the armchairs, waiting for Eliana to meet him. Eliana. The mother of his child and now, apparently, his friend.

Their conversation from a few days ago replayed in his head. He was unsure what had driven him to say that when he didn't mean it. He wanted to run his hands all over her sensual body in various activities that required both of them to take their clothes off.

Except he had to mean it. On a different level of consciousness he realised they needed a tried-and-true framework for their relationship with each other, so they wouldn't be stumbling in the dark while they figured out how to be parents. If his parents had chosen to think about him rather than their own desire and chaotic relationship, maybe he would have had a more stable home.

Diego wanted to do what was best for his child.

The thought still felt foreign to him. Having lived through such a volatile childhood, he'd never thought he would have a child himself. A baby meant stability, a partnership, a family built on trust and love. Two essential qualities he didn't know if he even possessed.

Time to find out, Diego told himself as he watched her come down the stairs.

His reaction to her was instant. The blood in his veins hummed with awareness as he repressed the urge to pick her up and carry her back to her room for a repeat show of that night several weeks ago.

'Olá,' he greeted her, his eyes running all over her body as she approached him.

She wore a dark red dress that sat tight around her torso and flared out into a wide skirt that accentuated the supple curve of her hips. Diego had to swallow the dryness spreading through his mouth as he imagined what the dress would look like in a pool around her feet.

'Bom dia...amigo.' She said the word 'friend' slowly, as if she was trying it on to see if it would fit.

He prayed that it would. That was the only way he saw to keep on being a part of her life, not just that of his child. Because for reasons Diego didn't dare to examine too closely, for fear of what he might see, he wanted to be a part of her life, too.

'You ready?' he asked after clearing his throat.

Looking at her drove blood to places that needed to remain dormant if they were to become friends. It wasn't as if Diego was particularly rich in friends. Although with his father's innumerable affairs he'd grown up with many half-siblings—some of them a very similar age to him. Being the woman she was, his grandmother had insisted on meeting all of her grandchildren, regardless of her son's stance on the issue, and had always maintained an open-door policy for any Ferrari child. That meant his childhood home had never been empty, but he'd had to grow up seeing his half-siblings' mothers involved in their lives while he only got to watch from afar.

He loved his half-siblings, and was glad to have them in his life, but he still sometimes struggled to see them because their mothers had chosen them, while he had become collateral damage in his parents' disastrous marriage.

His child would have a different life—he would make sure of that.

'What's the plan? Do you just want to have a bite here?' Eliana looked around.

The current passing back and forth between them was almost visible, making him feel ill at ease with their plan to keep things platonic.

'No, you've been living off hotel food for too long. Let me show you a special place.'

'Special?' Eliana asked with a raised eyebrow, but he only winked before he laid his hand on the small of her back to guide her to his car.

The touch was minuscule, so small that it could barely be called a touch, but the heat of it seared the tips of his fingers nonetheless, shooting small fires up his arm and into his chest. He bit the inside of his cheek to suppress the surging desire.

This was not how friends thought about each other.

'It's a nice place by the beach, but hidden enough so the tourists can't find it. I like to go there whenever I have the time—which isn't as often as I would like.'

A brief fifteen minutes later they pulled into a parking garage and walked a short distance to the beach, where they sat down at a small table right at the beachfront.

The expression of wonderment on her face was one of the most marvellous things Diego had seen in a while, and he had to bury his face in the menu so she wouldn't catch him staring at her with unabashed desire.

'See anything you like?' he asked, to distract himself from the unbidden heat rising in his chest.

'I don't know...' Eliana looked over the menu, a slight frown drawing the corners of her lips downwards. 'I like the sound of the steak sandwich, but lately red meat doesn't really agree with me. Or maybe it's the baby who doesn't like it. It's silly, but I think it's already developing its own tastes. As a doctor, I know that's impossible, but... I like to think it doesn't like meat so much. Maybe we're having a vegetarian.'

She paused, looking down at her menu with an intensity that almost made him chuckle. The embarrassment in her voice was incredibly sweet and sexy, and not warranted in any way. Their child was becoming more tangible with every passing day—it was only natural she would associate it with some characteristics.

A smile he had no control over curled his lips, and a warm sensation took tentative root in his chest as he enjoyed the purity of the moment they had just shared. Her care for their unborn child was extraordinary. Already it was so unlike the way his own mother had treated him, ripping him from his home with his *avozinha* whenever it had suited her.

Diego cleared his throat as he felt his chest suddenly constrict. No matter how intense the longing got he would not act on it. Passion faded; it always did. Their co-parenting relationship needed to be built on something more substantial and solid.

'Don't be embarrassed,' he said now, his voice a lot huskier than he'd intended it to be. 'Of course you're putting a lot of thought into what it might like and dislike. One day soon our baby will appreciate that.'

Eliana lifted her eyes off her menu to look at him, and the sparkling intensity of her gaze robbed him of his breath. 'Our baby... It's so strange to hear it, even though I know it's true. When I came to Rio I wasn't expecting anything like this.'

He raised an eyebrow at that. 'What *was* your plan?'

They had never really talked about it. Other than her desire to get back to Belo Horizonte in a few weeks.

'I don't make plans. In the past they haven't worked out for me, so I've stopped putting energy into planning things.'

The warmth in her voice had almost completely faded. Whatever lay behind her aversion for plans was clearly still a painful memory to her.

As someone who carried quite a few of those around himself, he knew better than to probe. If anyone did that to him he would shut them down instantly. Some borders weren't meant to be crossed, and his past was definitely one of them.

'Why is that?' he asked anyway, unable to stop himself.

He wanted to know her—the good things as well as the things that pained her. She was the mother of his child…a baby they'd decided they would bring up together. Surely that meant he needed to know something about her other than whatever Vanderson had told him about his long-estranged half-sister.

Eliana remained quiet, staring down at the glass of pineapple juice the waitress had just put down in front of her. She grabbed the little umbrella sticking out at the side of the glass, stirring the drink as she thought about her answer. Or rather thought about how she could best *not* answer him, he thought with a wry smile.

'Is it safe to assume you've heard all the rumours about Marco Costa's illegitimate daughter?' she asked, without raising her eyes from the glass.

Diego sighed. He abhorred the gossip that was spread in the corridors of Santa Valeria, especially when it involved Eliana. Being from a dysfunctional family himself, he knew exactly what kind of damage it could do to one's psyche, and it could just as easily have been him they gossiped about.

'Yes, I have,' he confirmed, and nodded although she wasn't looking at him.

'Good, so I can skip some things.' She laughed, but it sounded so unlike the laughter they had shared during their night together that Diego almost flinched at the bitterness.

'After my mother died in childbirth, my father did the bare minimum to raise me, leaving it to the hired help. Once I was old enough, he shipped me off to boarding school. A good one—and that's the reason why I was able to get into university—but the spoiled children of Brazil's elite weren't interested in befriending society's latest scandal child.'

She stopped to take a sip of her drink. Her voice had been calm and steady, but when she raised the glass to her lips he saw it shake, the ice cubes softly clinking against the glass. Her visible distress struck at something deep within him, and he reached out underneath the table, laying a supportive hand on her thigh.

'School was awful, and whenever I was home during the school break that was awful as well. Marco had a guest house set up as my apartment, so he didn't have to invite me into the house with his wife and son. Being all by myself, I dreamed of a different life…of parents who actually wanted me. I made so many plans, thinking that one day my father would come around. That one day he would see me as more than just a stain on his legacy. And I watched all those plans crumble into dust.'

Eliana heaved a deep sigh as she took another sip of her drink, finally lifting her eyes away from the glass to look at him. Her expression was guarded, and he couldn't see in it any of the emotion he had heard in her voice just a few seconds ago.

'Sorry, you didn't come here to listen to my sad childhood stories.'

'I'm glad you've said something. Plus, having problems with Marco Costa is something we have in common. You would have had a friend in Vanderson as well. He fought my corner when it came to dealing with Marco.'

He shrugged, trying to lighten the mood that had grown increasingly tense between them. His problems with Marco Costa were dwarfed by the cold and loveless childhood she had gone through.

That was something else they had in common, but he wasn't ready to share that part of himself with her. He didn't know if he ever would be. Probably not. Even friends didn't tell each other everything…

She smiled, but it didn't quite reach her eyes. 'I never saw much of Vanderson. I think our father didn't allow him near me. It's odd to think he disagreed with my father later on, when he obeyed him like that in the past.'

Diego shrugged, trying to defuse the tension still growing between them. He knew how much his best friend had regretted making the choices he had. But was it really his place to tell her that?

'I know Vanderson had to play by your father's rules because he held the keys to everything…hoarding power like he hoarded his wealth. Santa Valeria is a prime example of that. Marco chased profit and prestige above anything else, compromising the ability of his staff to do the good work they tried to do. Building those extravagant rooms, for example, was just one of many decisions he made that showed he was never about helping people.'

Eliana tilted her head to one side in an inquisitive look that kicked his pulse into overdrive. One minute she was pouring her heart out… the next she was sending him looks that made him want to forget about decency so he could have his way with her right here on the beach.

When that was the last thing he should want.

Not with a child between them.

There was too much at stake for any rash decisions, no matter how much his blood was burning for him to touch her.

It wasn't going to happen, and he'd better get that into his head now.

* * *

The words had tumbled out of her mouth as if she'd genuinely meant to say them—which she hadn't. Those memories—her father, the boarding school, the score of nannies—weren't meant to be brought to light and examined by anyone. Especially not by this man in front of her.

Eliana had enough problems resisting the fire of attraction sizzling between them without giving herself more reasons to like him. *Really* like him.

But something about Diego's compassionate eyes and the way he had laid his hand on her thigh as she poured her heart out had reassured her that she was in a safe space. That whatever she had to say he wouldn't judge her or make her feel silly for feeling like that. Not like the people she had grown up around, who had told her how lucky she was to be Marco Costa's daughter no matter how badly he treated her.

On the other hand, her half-brother had started to morph into a mystery in front of her eyes. He'd never been cruel to her when she was growing up, but he'd also never stood up for her, and he hadn't ever let on if he'd thought their father was mistreating her. She knew nothing about him as a person, and had always assumed that since he hadn't said anything to make her think otherwise he was one of his father's minions—

just like some of the other people she'd met at the hospital.

But Diego had started to paint a different picture of Vanderson. For the first time she began to wonder if he had been a victim of their father's manipulations just like her.

'You promised to tell me about Vanderson and how you two were involved. Did you know him well?' she asked, watching him with intent. She knew the two men were somehow connected.

A different kind of expression fluttered over Diego's face. Not contempt, but something else that hinted at a wealth of pain and complicated emotions.

'I knew him, yes. We both agreed that we couldn't let Marco run Santa Valeria the way he did, so we started working with each other.'

There had been a slight hesitancy in his voice as he spoke, as if he was choosing his words with deliberation.

'I noticed that Selma came in with instructions about her medical history written down,' she said. 'A note specifically asked her to come to Santa Valeria if she needed to, and to get them to page Vanderson if they had any questions.' She paused for a moment, tapping her finger against her chin as she followed her train of thought. 'I wondered if he was the one who initially treated her. She said she got her medicine from a free clinic, but that the doctor hadn't been there in a while. I think that might be because he died.'

'Not quite,' he said, and glanced away for a moment. 'Vanderson wasn't the one running the clinic, though he was involved. That note was from him. Your brother would help me with the free clinic in many different ways. One of them was covering patients if they came into A&E for treatments they normally received at the free clinic.'

Her heart stuttered in her chest as she processed his words. He had worked with her brother to bring free healthcare to people in need. A noble effort that was twisted by her unresolved feelings towards Vanderson. She had to admit that she didn't know what she had expected from him—only that what she had got wasn't enough. The picture she'd always had of him didn't quite fit in with caring about the disadvantaged people in the city.

'He helped you?'

Talking about her brother had unleashed a torrent of hurt inside her chest, but she wanted to know. What kind of man had he grown into? Had he regretted staying quiet?

Diego nodded, and she watched his expression as he scrubbed his hand over his clean-shaven face. He looked as if he was trying hard not to give anything away.

'He did, and I probably couldn't have done it without him. I bent a lot of rules so I was able to help people in my clinic, and Marco was suspicious when I…' He shook his head, his voice trailing off into a chuckle. 'I shouldn't be telling you this. You're still the new chief.'

'Oh? Why would you have reason to hide things? I already know you've convinced the emergency department staff to treat uninsured people.'

Her eyes narrowed on him as she thought about that. Was that what he'd been dancing around each time she'd felt him hesitate? How did his role at the Santa Valeria play into the free clinic?

Eliana's mouth fell open when she remembered their interaction with Selma. 'That's why you wanted to do the thoracentesis. Because you'd done it before.' She gasped, replaying the memory in her mind. 'Selma didn't let on a single thing!'

Diego had the decency to look somewhat embarrassed as a hesitant grin took over his face, robbing her of what little breath was left in her lungs.

'She's been coming to Santa Valeria long enough to know the drill whenever she meets a new doctor.'

'And Marco was riled up so much that he tried to fire you?'

Eliana remembered what Diego had told her. How good he had become at toeing the line to keep his job. Was that going to happen to them as well? Were they doomed to become antagonists at work while trying to figure out how to be good co-parents in private?

Was that something her mother had struggled with—co-parenting with a person who held all the power at work?

Diego hesitated, seeming to know what she was getting at. But she wanted to hear everything. A full confession.

'So we're doing it like this, huh?' he said.

She shrugged. 'I'm going to find out sooner or later, no? Might as well get it out there now, as we're clearing the air.'

'You wield a chief's power well, Ana,' Diego said as he leaned forward, resting his elbows on his thighs, giving her a view of the sculpted chest she remembered all too well.

A shiver ran from the top of her head all the way down to her toes, curling them inside her slingback sandals.

'From time to time I would spend some of my working hours in the free clinic rather than at the hospital. Only when there were other senior staff to help out in the orthopaedics department, and only when the patient load was manageable. Also, I would take the samples that pharmaceutical representatives brought and give them out at the clinic whenever someone needed something more than ibuprofen. That's how people like Selma keep their chronic conditions in check.'

He paused for a moment, his brow knit together.

'Most of the time we get general practice patients visiting the free clinic. Though the word has spread, and the lines outside get longer and the cases grow more desperate. Conditions that are very treatable under normal circumstances are exacerbated by the lack of healthcare available to the people living in the *favelas*.'

Diego leaned back in his chair, obscuring her enticing view down his button-up shirt again, and sighed.

'They're my people. I can't abandon them, no matter how difficult it is or how much trouble I might get into. Growing up, I watched people succumb to treatable diseases because families in the poorer parts of the city don't have adequate access to healthcare. So when I needed more hospital resources, I asked Vanderson for help.'

'You and Vanderson worked together to help the disadvantaged community?'

'We did. He would make sure that I got the time I needed with certain specialists. Marco didn't allow any kind of pro bono or community outreach work, but Vanderson was very good at packaging things in a way so that Marco could see a monetary benefit to it.'

Silence grew between them as Eliana took her time to process all the new things she had just learned about her brother, as well as Diego.

The waitress came by to ask about food, and Eliana realised that she hadn't even thought about it. She looked at Diego and he picked up on her silent plea, quickly glancing at the menu before ordering a variety of appetisers so they could have some bite-sized portions while they spoke to each other.

They were only just starting to get to know each other, and Eliana didn't want it to stop. The stranger she had met at a hotel bar on the day of her father's funeral was beginning to take shape right in front of her eyes. The more they spoke, the more she discovered about the compassion that drove him to be an excellent medical professional as well as a good man.

A *really* good man.

Their discussion had been so intense she hadn't noticed the low and persistent hum of awareness coursing through her body with every heartbeat. This was *not* good. She was supposed to find a healthy distance from him, so they could be co-parents without her head getting filled with mists of desire and longing every time she looked at him.

Maybe even friendship was a step too far.

What if being cordial acquaintances was all they could manage?

Eliana didn't know what she had hoped for today, but she knew that this strange closeness—the way her attraction was morphing into a deep longing in front of her eyes—wasn't it.

'So, what are you going to do now?'

Diego's low voice cut through her confusing contemplations and she looked at him with wide eyes.

'What do you mean?'

He chuckled. 'I've told you how I regularly misappropriate hospital resources to run my free clinic.'

'Oh, right…' That was the least of her concerns. Or else it was the root of her problem, depending on how she chose to look at it. It was his devotion to doing the right thing, helping the less fortunate, that turned the hot spear of desire piercing her chest into something larger and softer.

He was right. As the chief of medicine she should care about staff members disregarding the rules of the hospital. Whatever the reasons, his confession was a severe breach of protocol and should be met with some form of investigation.

Which was at direct odds with what she wanted to do. He was helping people…doing the right thing. Instead of investigating him and potentially reprimanding him, she wanted to help him. Make it official so he could stop sneaking around.

Was it that simple? Eliana wanted to believe so, although her feelings were getting entangled with business decisions. Did she like the idea because it was good for the hospital, or did she want to do it because she liked *him*?

'Will you show it to me?'

It was a terrible idea to get more involved with him than she already was. Their unplanned child was hard enough to deal with. If she dived further into personal things with him, it would take so much more effort to untangle herself.

Diego furrowed his brow, seemingly in agreement with her internal monologue. 'You want to visit the clinic?'

'Yes. Will you take me?'

He hesitated, his gaze shifting in and out of focus as he contemplated his answer.

'When do you want to go?'

'I'm not doing anything right now.'

CHAPTER SIX

DIEGO TRIED HIS best to watch her without staring as they entered Complexo do Alemão. They had left his car in the parking garage and waved down one of the yellow and green taxis so prominent in the streets of Rio de Janeiro. While the people in the neighbourhood knew him, and his practice, he still didn't dare drive up in anything that looked too expensive. He remembered what it had been like to grow up in the *favela*, and knew he wouldn't be making any friends by flaunting his wealth.

And safety was his primary concern with Eliana—much more than when he was on his own. He knew how to deal with people from his old neighbourhood, but she hadn't grown up here. He doubted that she had ever seen one of Rio de Janeiro's slums.

Her wide eyes as they drove up to the inconspicuous building that housed the clinic confirmed his suspicion. He tried to read her emotions as her expression fluttered and changed, but it was hard to guess what was going through her head.

Diego barely had any clarity in what was going through his own mind. He had shared so much of himself with her that he hadn't planned to—the things he had been doing in the free clinic most of all. She was the chief of medicine—the person holding the reins at Santa Valeria. He definitely shouldn't have volunteered the fact that he played fast and loose with the rules and hospital resources.

But something within him felt he owed her the truth—about his clinic, and also about himself. He still struggled to talk about Vanderson. The pain of his loss was dulled with every passing day, but every now and then it came rushing back to him, reminding him. Especially when it came to the plans they'd made to expand the clinic.

Was that why he had decided to tell Eliana? Did he want to bring her on board with those plans? She had asked him about her brother, and while he'd felt safe to share what they were doing here, he hadn't said how much he'd meant to him, scared that it might alienate him from her. When she'd spoken about Vanderson he'd seen a myriad of feelings flutter over her expression, and he had known there were a lot of unresolved feelings. Feelings that would now stay that way for ever.

No, he hadn't shared the clinic information with her for his own gain. That wouldn't have rung true within him. He had told her because he wanted her to know him—really know him. Which was a thought so terrifying Diego pushed it away.

He never got to know the women in his life because he didn't ever plan to spend more than one pleasurable night with them. Though Eliana would be in his life always, as the mother of his child.

But he could feel it running deeper than that—further than anything he had felt before. The rising heat inside his chest was messing with his head to the point where he had to use every ounce of self-restraint he still possessed not to sweep her up in his arms and carry her back to his place.

They were not meant to be more than what they were right now, though. Regardless of how electric her presence felt in his blood.

Diego shook his head, willing himself back into the present as he unlocked the door and held it open for Eliana. She walked through with a small smile on her full lips that instantly reignited the fire within him that he had just stamped out. Her light floral perfume drifted up his nose, making him long to have that scent lingering in his bedroom, the way it had back in the hotel all those weeks ago.

A different lifetime ago, when they hadn't been having a child together.

'Here we go. It's not much, but we don't really need much here. It's rare that anything complicated comes in.'

Diego had been expecting a comment about the state of the place. While it was clean, and furnished to his best abilities, it didn't even begin to compare to any facility her father had built in his long career as a medical professional.

But Eliana didn't comment on the clinic's appearance, her expression veiled, as she pointed at a closed door. 'Is that the exam room?'

'Yes. We technically have one on each side. Though currently only one is in use.'

She opened the door and walked through with Diego following on her heels. The exam room didn't look much different from the reception area. A sturdy table dominated the room, with two chairs standing next to it. There was an old-looking ultrasound machine in one corner, its protective covers gathering a layer of dust.

Eliana looked around with curious eyes, taking everything in as if she was taking stock. She walked past the exam table and looked at the closed cabinets lining the wall. Finally she turned around and leaned her hip against the table.

'I really don't know what I was expecting when you told me about it.'

Her voice sounded thick, and Diego crossed his arms in front of his chest, ready to defend his clinic. 'Do you have anything to say?'

She shook her head, her lavish red-brown curls bouncing around her face and making her look irresistible even in the poor lighting of the room.

'No, I'm impressed with your dedication to this place. You made it sound a lot worse than it is. I thought I'd find an MRI machine you'd stolen from the basement.'

Despite himself, Diego chuckled. 'I think you'd find an ambulance gone missing rather than one of the machines, if I ever dared to go that far.'

While he did technically steal—both his own time and his colleagues', and any pharmaceutical samples the companies left with him—he didn't consider it theft in a moral sense, although he didn't want to seem too blasé about it. Vanderson had given him permission for these things, bringing him close to but never across the hard lines.

But, going by the curious expression on her face, Eliana didn't seem to mind his clandestine activities. Was there still hope for the plans he had for the clinic?

'And you get a lot of people asking for help?'

she asked as her eyes drifted around the room once more.

'Why do you think I didn't turn on the light in the reception area? If someone sees the light on there'll soon be a queue of people outside.'

He sighed as he imagined the number of people he would see in the short blocks of time he spent here. Sometimes his *avozinha* would help him triage patients, so that he could attend to the most severe cases first.

The concern sparking in her face kicked something loose within Diego and his pulse quickened. Her next words almost undid him.

'There are really so many people that need treatment? Maybe we should turn the light on since it's the two of us here? I can help.'

Help. That was where her first thought went—to help all the people who needed her to cure them. She didn't ask him about the hours he spent here when he should be in the hospital. Nor did she want to know about the medication he had admitted to misappropriating from Santa Valeria's pharmacy. No, Eliana wanted to know how she could help the underprivileged people in his community.

Diego was speechless, gaping at her as he tried to find words for the feeling erupting in his chest.

Eliana shifted under his stare, raising her

brows in a half worried, half questioning gesture. 'What's wrong?'

'You must have received your generous heart from your mother, because there is no way it could have come from Marco,' he said, before he could think better of it.

He reached his hand out, wanting to fix the hurt he saw in her face without knowing how to do it. From the gossip echoing through the corridors of Santa Valeria he knew that her mother had been a nurse there before Marco had pushed her to move. The scandal of her getting pregnant by a married man who was also her boss was still something people liked to talk about—especially now that the result of this particular scandal owned the hospital.

Her brows reached even higher, transforming her expression into a look of surprise. 'Unfortunately I don't know much about her at all. I wish I could have met her. I'm sure she would have some advice for me about having an unexpected baby with a man who was a fling.'

'It'll be different for us,' he said without thinking, reaching for the first words that manifested themselves in his mind. 'Our baby will have a loving home no matter where it is.'

'Thank you, Diego. That means a lot.'

Her smile for him made his heart stop dead in his chest for a couple of seconds before it kicked back in, driving his blood to all the wrong places.

If she kept up like that she would prove to be his undoing. He felt himself slipping, wanting her right now, but also imagining having her working by his side at the clinic. Eliana cared about the people—his community—and she didn't even know them.

He'd be lucky to have a woman like that on his side. He could learn how to be different from the kind of man his father had been. Was there a world where they could be a family?

The softness in her eyes as they looked at him sparked a longing that pumped through his body with every heartbeat, spreading a heat he didn't know how to process.

He couldn't let himself hope for that. They had agreed not to. He didn't even know how to deal with what he was desiring in this moment. He should step away.

The thought echoed in his head even as he took a step towards her, drawn in by the look on her face.

'So, are you going to turn a blind eye on my clinic dealings?' He wanted to talk about something safe—something to distract him from the longing mounting within his chest.

'I don't know what to do about it. About anything, really. I wasn't ever supposed to be the chief of medicine at a hospital where everyone knows my story.'

He saw a shudder trickle through her body, and pain glimmered beneath the surface of her face.

'It doesn't surprise me that you had to do this behind my father's back. I never saw much of him when I was growing up. He couldn't even take care of the child he'd accidentally created. Sure, I was fed and clothed, but that was the end of it.'

Diego shook his head at the awfulness of that thought. He tried to imagine his *avozinha* rejecting any of his half-siblings for whatever reason, but she would never have gone in that direction. Just as he could never turn his back on his child, no matter the nature of its conception.

'I was raised by my grandmother. My parents weren't around much either,' he said, his mouth moving in a strange urge to share this part of himself with her—so she would understand that she wasn't alone in her conviction to be a better parent than those she'd had.

'What did they do?' She tilted her head to one side, her brown curls sliding over her shoulder, creating a picture of such pure feminine sensuality that he forgot what they were talking about for a fraction of a second.

'They were—are still—very unhappy together. My father would cheat on her, she would kick him out, then he would eventually come back to beg for her forgiveness. Their separations weren't easy. Lots of shouting, breaking things, accusations… And more often than not they'd forget that they had a son to look after.'

He shrugged when he saw the horror on Eliana's face. These memories had stopped bothering him a long time ago. They had done their damage on him, teaching him only chaos and volatility, to the point where he didn't know how to accept calm and love in his life.

'Whenever my dad strayed he would dump me at my *avozinha's* place. That went on for a couple of years until my grandmother put her foot down and kept me with her.'

'I'm sorry that happened to you,' she said with a frown of genuine concern for him.

He shrugged again. 'That's why I want to be better with…'

His voice trailed off as he struggled to finish the sentence. The word *us* echoed in his mind, but it would be a ridiculous thing to say to her. They were not anything that could remotely be considered an *us*. As small as that word was, it carried a lot of emotional depth that Diego wasn't prepared for.

'With…our baby?' Eliana prompted him, and he was relieved and disappointed that she hadn't said the word either.

'Yes,' he said, to distract himself from the emotions rising in his chest. 'We should have at least some idea of what we're doing before you leave.'

They were going to be parents, but that would be the extent of their relationship. They would never be more. Couldn't be more than that. He didn't know how.

With the small frown on her face deepening, she wove her fingers through each other, clasping her hands together. 'I know I've been avoiding this conversation, and I'm sorry about that. It probably didn't feel very nice…'

Diego had to smile at that. At least she was aware of what she had been doing. 'It didn't feel great, no,' he replied, letting her know the truth.

But when she hung her head he stepped closer to her, reaching out. He stayed his hand just before he made contact with her and felt heat radiate from her skin.

'This came as such a surprise…' she said. 'I needed some time to process things and—'

Their skin connected when Diego finally laid his hand on her bare shoulder, interrupting her mid-sentence. He noticed the small shudder run through her body the moment he touched her.

'You will never have to justify your choices to me, Ana. You had your reasons. The important thing is that we're talking now.'

* * *

Eliana's mouth fell open as she looked at Diego. The sincerity shining through his words sent hot sparks flying from behind her navel up her spine. Her cheeks flushed, and she could only imagine what kind of pink shade the fire rising inside her had chosen to show on her skin.

It wasn't his touch that sent a tremble through her extremities—though the memory of what his touch could do to her certainly contributed to the overall turmoil rising within her. It was the kindness in his eyes, the gentle understanding that lay underneath his words, that brought forth a whirlwind of emotion she wasn't prepared for.

This wasn't what friendship felt like. Her entire life Eliana had been short on friends, never really forming any kind of attachment to anyone. Yet she was still fairly certain that her feelings now ran a lot deeper than she wanted them to.

'Did you ever think about having a child?' Diego asked into the quiet.

Caught off guard, she gaped at him for a moment, her brain still busy with deflecting the feelings he was evoking in her. 'I… No, I didn't. My father not only drove my mother away from the one place she called home, he also failed to live up to his responsibilities after her death. I thought that once the right person showed up in my life I would tackle family planning with him…hope they would be able to teach me the qualities I lacked from growing up the way I did. But…'

Her voice faltered, and she looked up at Diego when his hand slid down her arm, his fingertips grazing her skin and raising the fine hair on it. His eyes were shining with sympathy, as if he knew the pain weaving itself through her words.

And today she had learned that he did know her pain. Hearing how his parents had dumped him, with no regard to what that might do to him, had broken her heart. He'd been through a lot more than he let on, but was shrugging it off as if it were not a big deal. No wonder he felt so strongly about his part in their child's life.

'What about you?' she asked. Growing up like that must have left a mark on him, too.

Diego stayed quiet for a moment, his eyes drifting away from her face and to his hand, which was still gently caressing the skin of her arm, sending small shivers down her body with every sweep of his fingers.

'I didn't ever think I had what it takes for fatherhood. Still don't—not with how much of a failure my own father has been. A happy family is a foreign concept to me. I don't know how to make one myself, so I never indulged in any thought of having a relationship or children.'

His voice took on a strange quality, as if all of

a sudden he had drifted miles away. He seemed to notice, for he cleared his throat.

'That doesn't mean I won't be there for my child every step of the way. I fully acknowledge my responsibility in all of this, and I'm not going to shy away from it.'

An unusual disappointment gripped Eliana. She tried to shove it away almost immediately. She shouldn't be disappointed that he wasn't interested in any kind of attachment—the opposite, really. While deep down inside she wanted to find a person to spend the rest of her life with, this wasn't how it was going to happen—just because he felt a sense of obligation towards her.

'Why do you say that?' she asked, though she wasn't sure what drove her to dig deeper. Somehow she simply wanted to know more about him for her own selfish reasons, if nothing else.

Diego seemed taken aback by her question. 'Do you not want me to be there every step of the way?'

'No, I meant… Why do you believe you don't know how to be happy with someone?'

A flash of something intangible streaked across his expression. An ancient pain and vulnerability. Eliana held in a breath at the sight, as if she was standing face to face with a precious creature that would skip away at any moment if she made a wrong move. If she remained still enough would he open up to her?

'That's a complicated question to answer,' he said after some deliberation.

Despite his words implying a need to distance himself, he stepped closer and leaned his hip against the exam table she now sat on. The increased proximity sparked a fire under her skin, raising the fine hair on her arms.

'Try me. I'm pretty smart,' she said. Her voice was a lot raspier than she'd intended it to be, and she resisted the urge to clear her throat. Maybe he hadn't noticed.

His eyes narrowed, and the gaze gliding down to her lips told her that he definitely had noticed the huskiness of her tone.

'My father took vast liberties with his wedding vows, and instead of seeing him for the man he was my mother kept returning to him every time he came crawling back. I grew up watching my half-siblings—the by-products of my father's countless affairs—have a relationship with their mothers. Those women had been betrayed—just like my mother. But they hadn't shifted the blame to their children. No, I was the only Ferrari child who'd ruined his mother's life just by being alive.'

He scoffed, turning his face away from her and staring at an undefined point at the wall. The pain resurfaced on his expression so slowly that Eliana was sure he was fighting himself on the inside. But he didn't have to hide—not from her. She knew that hurt...had experienced some of it herself. Her father had resented her for existing.

The moment she saw Diego's face contort again she felt her heart make a decision before her brain could caution her to think twice. She reached out to touch him, laying her hand on his cheek and drawing his eyes back to her.

Her thumb rested on his sculpted cheekbone, brushing against it with a slight hesitancy, testing the waters. His expression went blank the moment her hand connected with his skin, nothing but a subdued spark remaining in those dark brown eyes.

'You're too hard on yourself,' she said in a low voice. 'You aren't turning away from your responsibilities. That's something your father would do, right?'

Eliana wasn't sure why she was consoling him, or what had led her to ask such personal questions in the first place. Her upbringing had lacked any parental figure to learn from, making her believe she was missing the special 'something' children got from watching their parents. Why was she so adamant about Diego criticising himself unfairly when she thought the same thing about herself?

But despite her own doubts Eliana's words

seemed to reach him—for his eyes grew wide in bewilderment. It was as if he had never thought about his own actions, with his head too wrapped up in what he believed to be true about himself.

Eliana's heart stopped beating for a second when he moved his hand up to his face, placing it on top of hers. He leaned in, and the intensity in his eyes was reminiscent of the night they'd met. The night they had made their baby.

'I'm not the kind of man you think I am,' he whispered in a low voice as he got closer to her face.

He slid her hand off his cheek and over his mouth, brushing her palm with a soft kiss that shot a flare of flames through her system, to settle in the depths of her core.

She wanted to move, to escape this situation. She was getting dangerously close to making the same mistake again. Diego had an incredible talent whereby he could bypass her defences with little effort on his part. Make her feel she wanted him—which she definitely didn't. Shouldn't, really.

Not when there was a child in the middle of it all.

'What kind of man do I think you are?'

'A man who is capable of giving more than I've already shown you. A man who sticks around.' He paused for another moment, his face so close to hers that she felt his breath on her skin. 'I can tell you now that I'm not your happily-ever-after, so don't waste your feelings on me.'

His words hit her with an unexpected ferocity that created an uncomfortable pinch in the pit of her stomach. Was that what she was looking for? Someone who stuck around no matter what? Her father certainly hadn't, leaving her with the bare minimum of attention to survive and little else. Eliana had never been anyone's priority, which had led to her never feeling quite settled wherever she was—never feeling safe.

Did she want that from Diego? Permanence?

She swallowed her emerging feelings as he looked at her. 'We both agreed this would be for the best,' she said, 'so I'm not going to turn around and demand a romantic relationship from you. I want to know you because you're the father of my child, not because I'm pining for you.'

Her words stood as a stark contrast to their actions. Their faces were inching closer to one another as they seemed lulled into a sensual cloud of their explosive desire for one another.

'Good, I'm glad we settled that—so I can do this,' he said, with a grin that brought her blood to a boil inside her veins.

'Do wha—?'

The rest of the word didn't make it past her

lips, for Diego had closed the remaining distance between them and pressed his mouth against hers in a kiss she had been waiting for since the day they'd met again.

Her flight instinct melted away under his gentle yet probing touch as his hands wandered over her neck, his fingers creating hot fires underneath her skin as they moved.

This was not what she'd had in mind when they'd spoken about getting to know each other better. But this kind of getting to know him—despite the vagueness of his words—felt so right. She had glimpsed something of him beyond the detached surgeon he let the rest of the world see. It had awakened a need within her that reached far beyond the initial desire that had brought them together so many weeks ago. Could there be something more to their connection?

The thought barely took shape in her mind as Diego's hands slipped to the back of her head, his fingers weaving themselves through her hair and gently pulling her head back, deepening the kiss as her lips parted, receiving the warmth of his tongue that was sending a shudder through her body.

Her hands clutched at him, holding on to his strong shoulders and pulling him even closer into their sensual embrace. Whatever hesitation Eliana might have felt when she'd agreed to meet him this morning it had melted away now, under the power of his words and the desire his touch evoked in her.

They had both stated their boundaries. Neither of them was interested in a long-term commitment, and they didn't believe in staying together just for the sake of their child. So there was no danger in giving in to the flood of passion cascading through her body, right?

The stakes were clear. She would still walk away from here as soon as her business was done.

Why not enjoy the moment?

He knew he shouldn't give in to the boiling desire bubbling in his blood, but he could not resist the temptation that was Eliana. The second he had seen her in the hotel lobby Diego had known he was fighting a losing battle to keep his hands to himself. Though his intentions had been pure—and he really did want to ease into some sort of friendship with her that would help them raise their child together—he'd soon felt the pull of her unbelievable sensuality tugging at him whenever he'd been able to observe her with her guard down.

Her questions had caught him off guard. While he could acknowledge that closeness would come with getting to know the other person better, he still wasn't sure what had urged him to disclose as much as he had. Other than Vanderson, no one knew about his parents and what kind of damage they had left on him.

His confession about his past had broken the last barrier that had seemed to be keeping his mounting lust in check, and a few moments later he'd stopped resisting and let go of control, his body taking over while his mind was still busy catching up with what they had discussed.

Now Diego crushed her against him, his hands roaming over her back, dipping into every curve of her body and exploring each angle as they were locked in a kiss that spoke of the passion both of them felt simmering between them. Soft moans escaped from her throat, muffled by his own mouth. The vibration of the sound penetrated his skin and set his blood on fire, as if someone had swapped it with a flammable liquid. All his blood rushed to the lower half of his body, pooling in his groin as Eliana's hands slipped under the seam of his shirt, grazing over the skin of his stomach.

But they were still in the clinic—not the best place to do what they were both dying to do… again. It cost him a lot more effort than he'd thought possible to rip his mouth from hers.

A soft gasp escaped Eliana's lips when he drew away, her hands immediately going limp and letting go of the fabric of his shirt. She looked shocked, as if she had just caught up with reality.

'This might not be the right place,' he said when she remained quiet.

There was a small apartment above the clinic, where he sometimes stayed in a pinch, if he was too exhausted to drive. But the look on her face was changing between passion and confusion.

He didn't want to let the moment disappear like that—even though his rational side urged him to take a break and retreat. Their lives were already messy enough…maybe he shouldn't add more sex into the mix.

Yet the beast inside his chest still roared, demanding to fulfil the promise of passion hanging between them. Even now he could see her chest heaving, her flushed cheeks showing the heat coursing through her veins.

'This used to be my grandmother's house,' he said, to fill the silence between them. 'We bought it from her to have a place for our clinic.'

Eliana looked at him, with a sudden curiosity in her face that he hadn't expected. 'Who?' she asked.

Diego stared back with a blank expression, not comprehending the question. 'Who…?' he repeated with a puzzled inflexion.

'You said "we". You and who?'

And just like that the fire in his veins died as if someone had doused him with icy water.

He hadn't even realised that he still thought of the clinic as a shared effort between him and Vanderson until she had pointed it out. Even though it had been almost two months since the funeral, the unexpected loss of his friend kept creeping back into his consciousness at the oddest moments.

'Huh… I didn't even notice I'd said that,' he mumbled, and gave in to a sudden urge to share his thoughts. 'I initially started this clinic, but it didn't take long for Vanderson to get involved. He was the one to handle his father whenever we needed to bring one of our patients from here to Santa Valeria. You have your own opinion about him, and I'm not going to excuse anything he may have said or done. But your brother…' Diego hesitated for a moment, not sure how he wanted to end that sentence. 'He cared. And I know he struggled with how he had let things happen.'

'Were you close to him?' Her voice had adopted a strange quality, as if she was afraid of his answer.

What would be worse for her?

The tension of their desire for each other had left them with the mention of Vanderson, to be replaced by an unusual stillness. They were still somewhat intertwined, with her hands lying on his chest while he gripped her hips and held her close to him, their faces only inches from each other.

'Yes,' he said, watching her face for any kind of clue to how that answer would make her feel, waiting for a reaction from her.

She opened her mouth to speak, but a loud knock on the door interrupted her. A moment later the door opened, and female voices filtered through the air.

Eliana went stiff in his arms and immediately backed away from him, freeing herself from his grasp.

'Diego, *você está aqui?*' a familiar voice shouted from the reception area, and he got up with a sigh.

'Yes, I'm here, *Avozhinha.* But we're not open right now.' He glanced at Eliana with an apologetic look. 'Sorry, I'll deal with this real quick.'

He stood up to greet his grandmother. But as he moved towards the door she walked through it—and with her a tired-looking woman pushing a wheelchair with a young boy sitting in it.

'Oh, hey, Miguel. I wasn't expecting you here so soon,' Diego said when he recognised his patient. He went down into a squat to greet the boy, and in a gesture that was more habit than anything else started examining the stump where his left leg had used to be. 'Are you okay? What brings you here?'

'I was just in the area to bring Layla some

food,' his grandmother said. And then her eyes fell onto Eliana, who had got up from the table and moved closer with a curious expression. 'Oh, I didn't know you had company.'

'This is Eliana, the new chief of medicine at Santa Valeria,' Diego said as he checked on the boy's leg.

Miguel had outgrown his previous leg quite a while ago, and the ill-fitting prosthetic had caused some damage to his skin and muscle tissue. The scarring was not very visible, but Diego felt it under his fingers. They were lucky that Miguel was so young, or his scars might have prevented him from fitting a new prosthesis.

'How wonderful! Does that mean we can fit Miguel's leg soon?' Layla, Miguel's mother, looked hopeful at his grandmother's words, and both of them looked to Eliana for an answer.

Her eyes went wide with surprise, and she looked at him. 'What's the problem with the leg?'

Diego gestured her to move closer, and had to suppress a shudder when she knelt down next to him, as the floral scent of her perfume danced around his nose, robbing him of his concentration.

'He's outgrown his old prosthetic leg. We see that a lot with patients who lose a limb at a young age. Unfortunately, Miguel doesn't have the privilege of regular check-ups with an orthopaedic specialist, to see when the prosthetic leg has grown too small. The damage to his soft tissue is not too stark, but still noticeable.'

Eliana looked at the boy with a small smile on her face. '*Olá*, Miguel, I'm Eliana, and I'm a doctor, too. Are you okay with me examining your leg?'

He nodded, and a moment later she wrapped both of her hands around the small stump where his leg had used to be.

'Hmm, I see what you mean,' Eliana said as she withdrew her hands and looked at Diego, concern etched into her features. 'Can we bring him in? I don't think you have the right facilities here.'

'I...' He hesitated.

The last couple of days he had been making clandestine plans with the paediatric specialist on his team to get Miguel the help he needed. Something that wasn't exactly above board, as he would technically be misappropriating hospital resources to help a patient who couldn't afford treatment.

But Eliana's reaction to this moment was one he hadn't dared to hope for earlier, when he had asked her what she would do now that he'd shown her the clinic. She didn't care about the price tag—she just wanted to help. That fact made the beast roar inside his chest again. If this was her first reaction to seeing a patient in need maybe there were other things they could do together. Maybe even…

'Yes, with your permission I would like to get my team on this case. I've done what I can on my own, but I've reached a point where I need more help,' he said.

Eliana nodded. 'Good, let's get him admitted right now. The fitting will take a couple of days, and Miguel will probably also need some physical therapy before we can release him again.' She walked over to the examination table where she'd left her tote bag and retrieved her phone from it. 'I'll ask my assistant to send over an ambulance.'

'Wait, I can't leave. My work…' Layla looked at his grandmother and then at Eliana, lifting her hands in a helpless gesture. 'I can't miss work or I won't be able to afford any of this.'

Diego watched as Eliana walked over to the woman, laying a hand on her arm to pacify her.

'I don't want you to worry about money. Santa Valeria has a fund for cases like this, so you won't have to pay a single *real*. Miguel needs some special treatment before we can fit his new leg. It will take a few days, but I will ensure someone sends you regular updates. Diego will be supervising his case personally, so you have nothing to worry about while Miguel is away.'

She tilted her head to look at him, and he nodded. 'You know I'll take good care of him, Layla.'

The woman still looked frightened, but she agreed to their plan with a nod. When he had first seen Miguel he had made sure to let her know they were looking at quite a lot of work if they wanted him to regain full mobility with his prosthetic leg.

'It's so nice to meet you, Eliana. My grandson tells me you came to Rio on your own. Why don't you join us for the *churrasco* I'm hosting at my house next weekend? Diego's sister has just graduated, and we're celebrating.'

His *avozinha*'s words launched him back into reality, and his eyes went wide in surprise. What had she just said?

'Oh, thank you, but I couldn't possibly impose on you like that when I don't even know your granddaughter.'

Eliana smiled, but he could see the hint of hesitance bubbling in the corners of her mouth.

'Avozinha, *por favor*… This is my new chief you're talking to,' he said in a low voice. The warning in his words was clear, and he knew his grandmother would make him regret that tone later on.

'Even more important to make a good impression and invite her to dinner, then. I'm not having any arguments about this. With her helping my friend Layla the way she is, that is the least I can do, *querida*.'

Márcia waved her hand in a way he knew all too well. She had made up her mind, and it was going to happen. Which put Diego in a difficult situation. Despite their best intentions, they hadn't got any closer to making decisions about their child today. The only thing they'd managed to do was entangle themselves further into the mess they had started two months ago.

Diego knew better—knew that he shouldn't let his need overpower his rational side. Yet all he could think about was how fast he could get everyone out of here so they could pick up things right where they'd left off. Preferably upstairs in a comfortable bed.

'Well, if I'm not imposing…thank you, I would love to come.'

Eliana glanced at Diego with an expression he couldn't quite read. She looked apologetic, but there was something else mixed into it as well. Was she excited to be invited to his family's barbecue?

'Of course, dear. Vanderson used to come by all the time—everyone will be excited to meet his sister.'

The short howl of a siren interrupted his

avozinha, and a moment later the ambulance pulled up to the house.

'There's our ride,' Eliana said to Miguel, with a smile that looked plastered on.

The mention of her brother had made her freeze up, and Diego hissed internally at his grandmother's careless words. He had told her enough about Eliana that she should have known better than to mention Vanderson. Especially since they had only really started to speak about his relationship with her brother today, and hadn't got far into the conversation before they had been interrupted.

'Are you coming with us to the hospital?' she asked.

Diego stared at Eliana for a second, fighting the disappointment that was spreading through his chest. He had been hoping they would have a moment alone so they could talk. They had so much to talk about. His relationship with her brother… The child they had yet to tell anyone about… Their kiss…

But he understood this request was coming from the chief of medicine and not his…his *what*, exactly? She shouldn't be his anything, yet the ambiguity of it tightened his chest as if someone was wrapping a rope around it.

'Yes, of course.'

Miguel had been cleared for treatment, and that had to be his highest priority at that moment. No matter how much he wanted to revisit that moment from an hour ago, when they had been intertwined once more.

CHAPTER SEVEN

ELIANA LOOKED AT herself in the floor-length mirror of the hotel room, turning to one side and scrutinising her profile. Her hand lay on her stomach, searching for an indicator of her baby, but everything remained flat and undetected. This wasn't surprising. She was only at the end of her second month, and most pregnancies didn't start to show until the second trimester.

By then, she hoped to be back in Belo Horizonte, far away from Diego and that fire in his eyes that she wanted to get lost in.

'I'm blaming you for this, little one,' Eliana mumbled at her stomach, even as she felt a prickle of arousal trickle down her spine, settling in her core in an uncomfortable pinch.

Her hormones made this whole friendship endeavour with the incredibly hot Dr Ferrari a lot harder than she wanted it to be. Or at least she used her hormones as a convenient excuse to cling to, because she could hardly believe that she would have been so careless of her own volition. To make out with Diego when they had both agreed to take a step back from the passion sizzling between them.

She let herself fall on the bed with a sigh and grabbed her phone to stare at the screen. She read the message she had typed out to Diego, giving her apologies and telling him that she couldn't attend the party after all.

That was what a smart person would do. Untangle herself from any more situations that weren't strictly necessary and keep any and all conversations centred around one of two things: their work or their child.

But the voice urging her to send the message was weak, drowned out by the mounting curiosity inside her. Despite things not going as planned, Eliana had glimpsed a part of Diego that lay beyond the thick wall he hid behind, and from his reaction she knew he rarely let anyone see that part of him—if ever.

Diego had suffered a lot more than he let on, and even more than that he seemed to think that he was damaged beyond repair. She wanted to know more about him—both about his family and his relationship with her late half-brother. He had hinted that they'd had a close relationship…something his grandmother Márcia had confirmed when she'd said that he would have been invited to the barbecue were he still alive.

Would she and Diego be able to get over their electrifying attraction and be the kind of friends they wanted to be? Diego had shown her a different side of himself—one she understood all too well. And even though she knew he was nothing like her father, the comparison kept creeping up into her brain, making her wonder.

Had her mother at some point believed Marco to be committed to raising their child together?

Even if Diego's commitment was solid, would he really make the time as he'd promised?

Losing her mother even before her own life had begun and being raised by a rotation of employees without ever knowing a loving touch, Eliana wanted more than anything else to be someone's priority. Wanted nothing to be more important than what they had together.

Diego had already picked what was most important to him—his community. She wouldn't change that, and didn't want to either. His commitment to helping the disadvantaged had opened her heart to him more than she cared to admit.

But they couldn't be together. Not when they wanted such vastly different things in life. Diego strived to be of service to his people—those who had brought him up when his parents had failed him. Eliana, on the other hand… For once, she wanted to matter. And if Diego had to split his attention it would be for the sake of their child, and not because of some misguided romantic feelings for her.

'Okay, we can go and meet your extended family. But only if you promise to behave, young one,' Eliana said to her unborn child. 'No mood swings, no hormones that make Mamãe feel things—are we clear?'

She waited in the quiet for a moment, feeling her connection to her child on such a deep level she was almost overwhelmed. It had been nothing more than an accident, and yet her chest was filled with love and affection for this tiny being already. She didn't know how she could have lived her life without that feeling.

'Good, then let's go and meet Papai.'

Diego had texted her the address of his grandmother's place earlier in the week, with a note saying that he'd understand if she didn't want to attend. She had wondered if that was his way of asking her not to come, but the look on his face when he opened the door for her completely wiped that thought from her brain.

Because the way he looked at her, his eyes ablaze with need the second his gaze fell on her, made Eliana's knees almost buckle.

Or was that her needy mind playing tricks on her? Making her want to believe Diego wanted her as much as she was burning for him?

'I'm glad you're finally here,' he said in a

low voice, and Eliana let out a breath she hadn't known she had been holding in.

'You are?' she asked, in spite of herself and her desire to make her composure appear resolute.

'Of course. Talking to you will give me a good excuse to avoid all my half-siblings. Ever since the funeral they've been overbearing.' He paused for a moment and laughed. 'It also means I can stop guarding the door.'

Eliana laughed with him, not letting the information he had just shared show on her face. Vanderson's death had hit him hard enough that his entire family was worried about him. Not for the first time she wondered how the two men had found their way into each other's lives.

'Before I let you in, I must warn you. Almost the entire Ferrari clan is here—including spouses and children. Enough people that I hope we'll become invisible. My family is also incurably nosy, so if they pester you let me know and I'll be your shield.'

Eliana had to laugh at his grave warning. 'Wait—how many half-siblings do you have?'

'Ten,' he said, and stepped aside to let her in.

The moment she walked across the threshold the muffled noise she had been hearing intensified around her.

'Ten?' She tried her best to keep the surprise out of her voice, but knew she hadn't quite managed to do so when she caught a strange expression fluttering across his face. It wasn't shame, but something akin to it. Was he embarrassed about his siblings?

'I told you my father was rather liberal with his interpretation of his wedding vows.'

This time she had no problem understanding his mood. A bitter edge wove itself through each word, and his resentment towards his father clear as day. Clearly while still married to Diego's mother, he'd had ten additional children out of wedlock.

'He's not here tonight, is he?' she asked, even though she thought she knew the answer already.

Diego laughed in derision. 'Not a chance in the world. He might be Vanessa's father, but I would be surprised if he even knew that she's just finished university. Ignacio Ferrari is not exactly...*involved* in any of our lives.'

'Good. Your siblings seem happy enough without his bad energy,' she said, with a playful chuckle underpinning her voice. 'And from the sounds of it, our new *princesa* will have enough aunts and uncles that she won't need grandfathers.' She patted her flat stomach affectionately and noticed Diego's eyes dart to her hand.

'*Princesa?* It's been a long time since my obstetrics rotation, but surely you can't know that at this point?'

Eliana shrugged. 'I'm only guessing from the feeling she's giving me.'

Some of the humour she had got to know so well over the last couple of weeks entered his eyes again. She much preferred this Diego over the one agonising about his painful past.

'Feeling? *Querida*, you are a woman of science. Next thing you'll tell me you've had the tarot read to determine the future of our child.' He tried to sound outraged, but his wide grin gave his true feelings away.

Her reply never crossed her lips, for a fire had suddenly burst to life right behind her navel, pumping heat through her entire body until her fingers felt tingly.

Querida.

A perfectly innocent endearment of familiarity. People used it all the time, to the point where it meant very little. But hearing it from his lips had catapulted her desire for this man in front of her up to the surface, despite her best efforts to keep her growing feelings buried.

He wasn't interested in her. No, he was here only because they were having a child together. It was their child that was behind all his interactions with her. She needed to get that into her head.

'Are you okay?' he asked when she remained

quiet, but before she could say anything they were interrupted by a woman's voice calling for Diego.

'Diego! The meat is almost ready. Can you…? Oh, who do we have here?'

Eliana saw that the woman stood almost as tall as Diego when she stopped next to them, and although her ebony skin stood in stark contrast to Diego's tawny hue, the high cheekbones and bright brown eyes immediately gave them away as siblings.

'This is Eliana Oliveira, the new chief of medicine at Santa Valeria. Avozinha thought it appropriate to invite my boss to the *churrasco*.'

His sister raised her eyebrows to look at him with a scepticism that intrigued Eliana. She didn't seem to believe him.

'She must have seen you two together if you got an invitation. You know Vovo doesn't like it that you always come to our family dinners on your own.' She turned to face Eliana. 'It's nice to see Diego has made a friend. I'm Gloria, his little sister.'

The woman stepped closer and air-kissed each of Eliana's cheeks before stepping away again.

'It's nice to meet you,' she replied, feeling a redness coat her cheeks at the way Gloria had emphasised the word 'friend'. Up until this moment she hadn't even thought about what her presence here might look like to other people. Would they think something was going on between them?

But there was, wasn't there? The memories of their kiss rushed back into her consciousness and she pushed them away.

'Well, don't hide away the first person you've brought home since Vanderson. Let me give her a tour.'

Eliana looked at Diego for a moment. He gave her a look of equal uncertainty before his sister took her by the arm.

By the time they sat down for dinner she had met every single Ferrari sibling, as well as their spouses and children.

Diego had groaned each time one of his family members had started to ask too many questions, or insinuated that he was usually not seen with a woman. But although he seemed exhausted by all their thinly veiled suggestions about their relationship status, Eliana saw the genuine connection he had with all of his siblings. Despite his father's wrongdoings, somehow his offspring had pulled through to the other side, forming a unique and beautiful family unit where they cared for each other.

Everyone seemed beyond excited to meet Eliana, which was a new feeling for her. No one had ever expressed this kind of enthusiasm on meeting her before. And what confused her the most was that they seemed excited she was here simply because Diego had brought her. Even though they didn't know anything about her, or their relationship, they wanted to get to know her.

It was that that caused a painful twinge in her chest. She had never known what it was like to be part of a family dynamic. Would she be able to give her child everything it needed even though she didn't know the first thing about family herself? Or was that where Diego came in?

She glanced to where he was sitting next to her, listening to the partner of one of his siblings. He seemed to know how to form close bonds much better than she did. His father hadn't spread his toxicity to his children, though clearly not for lack of trying. In Diego's interactions with his siblings she could see some hesitancy, though—as if he didn't dare let any of them get too close.

But they were all gossiping and laughing with each other without a care in the world. They had managed to pull through their rocky childhood. How come Diego believed himself incapable?

They wrapped up after dessert by toasting the woman of the evening, Vanessa, who had apparently just finished veterinary school, and then the Ferrari clan broke out into smaller groups again.

A warm sensation trickled down her spine when Diego laid his hand on her shoulder, prompting her to look up into his breathtakingly handsome face.

'Let's find a quiet spot. I think we both might have had enough questions and inquisitive looks.'

The smile spreading across his lips made her knees feel soft for a moment, forcing her to reach for the hand he was offering her. The contact didn't help with the weakness, and her heart was sent into overdrive when he didn't let go of her hand as they walked away from the noise to the other side of the garden from where the table had been set.

Only when they turned a corner did he let go, and point at a periwinkle-blue wooden bench that stood against the house's exterior wall. They sat down together, and the few inches of space between them felt like a cavern as Eliana raised her eyes to look at him.

Though she had enjoyed the conversation, and all the questions thrown at her, she'd noticed one particular topic was missing.

'You haven't told anyone about the pregnancy?'

'No, I haven't.' Diego stared straight ahead

for a couple of breaths. 'I felt like that wasn't a decision I should make alone.'

He hadn't wanted to make that decision on his own because they were in this together, she thought. Diego—though still surrounded by thick walls and shrouded in mystery—considered them a team.

Not a couple—he had insisted on that previously, and Eliana had forced herself to agree, even if she found resistance inside her. But a faint voice in her head kept calling out to him, tempting her to forget about the boundaries she had set.

He had made her a priority in that moment. Thinking about how she would feel before telling people news that was just as much his as it was hers.

'Thank you, I appreciate that,' she replied into the quiet, and smiled at him, giving herself permission to feel the warmth pooling in her stomach despite knowing that it couldn't ever be more than a fleeting emotion. But he cared about her—something she was not used to from anyone. Maybe she could trust him with more than she was giving him credit for...like her thoughts about Vanderson.

'I want to know more about my brother. You said you were close.' The words tumbled from her lips before she could decide against them. 'You still haven't told me much about him.'

He'd been near invisible in her life, but maybe Diego could shed some light on him. Had he grown up regretting his past actions?

The pain fluttering over Diego's face made her regret speaking those words, but as she took a breath, ready to take them back, he nodded.

'I know I've been avoiding the topic. His death was so…unexpected. It still leaves me numb sometimes. But you never had the chance to meet the real Vanderson, and I want you to know about your brother. How he opposed your father and how much he wanted to be reconciled with you.'

Reconciliation. A concept Eliana had thought about a lot when it came to her brother. And apparently, he had thought about it too. But then why had he never reached out?

She put those thoughts away for now. There were other things she wanted to know first. 'How did you meet? You didn't know him as a boy, or I would have seen you around.'

Diego shook his head. 'I met him during our mandatory military service. We were both training as medics, planning on attending med school afterwards. Our assignments often put us together, and we spoke a lot about what we wanted to do…how we planned on helping the less fortunate. Me because I had grown up poor, and him because he had seen what greed had done to his father's hospital.'

He paused for a moment, his hand balling into a tight fist, and Eliana resisted the urge to reach out to him.

'We decided we wanted to make a difference—which was when our idea for a free clinic in my old neighbourhood was born. Through his…your father, Vanderson was well connected, and he recommended me for a position at Santa Valeria once I had finished my medical training. We were waiting for Marco to retire, so Vanderson could take over. And he was also waiting for your father's retirement before reaching out to you.'

Eliana's mouth went dry and she swallowed hard. 'What had my father's retirement to do with Vanderson reconnecting with me?'

Diego sighed, a rueful smile on his face. 'Marco was a sad and spiteful person. From a young age Vanderson was forbidden to talk to you, and even after your brother had become an adult Marco threatened to disown him if he went against his wishes. Vanderson would have been ready to take that chance had it not been for the ownership of the hospital.'

This was information she had never heard before, and it stood in direct contrast to what she had believed to be true almost all her life. She had believed her brother to be her father's minion at worst, and apathetic at best.

'He really wanted to know me?' She didn't

know why she'd asked that question. It had sounded so desperate.

'Not being strong enough to be the brother you needed when you were growing up was the biggest regret in his life, and it pains me that he'll never get the chance to make it right.'

That confession took all the remaining air out of her lungs. She had never known what kind of person her brother was. A small part of her had always hoped that he would want to know her, but with each day that went by without her hearing from him, her hope had grown slimmer.

'Did you know he was married and had a child?' Diego asked, and grinned when she shook her head. He had his own family? Maybe those were the people the lawyers had spoken about. Marco and Vanderson's estates were closely linked. The estate lawyer had told her that there were other, unnamed beneficiaries of the will, which had made the estate complex enough to force Eliana into staying in Rio longer than she'd intended.

He reached into his pocket, retrieved his phone and unlocked it with a swipe before going through his camera roll.

'His husband's name is Alessandro, and their daughter's name is Daria. He owns a recreational facility near the beach, renting out surfboards and such. Daria has just turned five.

They adopted her when she was a couple of months old.'

The picture had been taken on a gorgeous summer day, with blue skies unfolding behind them. Diego, Vanderson and his husband plus child were seated at a round table, all of them smiling at the camera that, judging from the angle, Diego must have been holding.

Eliana's throat suddenly felt tight as she looked at the picture. It was serene, and full of the affection those four people had shared with each other. But more than that it made her realise that she had something she'd never known.

'I have a niece? And a brother-in-law?'

Her voice sounded strained in her own ears as she struggled with the sudden revelation. She had never even thought that her brother might have been married and had children.

It reinforced once more how close Diego had been to her late brother. How much did he already know about her? Was he nodding along as if he was hearing new information when he had already heard it from his best friend?

'So, did Vanderson tell you about my childhood? You must have already known about me before we met.'

Her voice was free of accusation, but she saw that he winced, nonetheless.

'He didn't tell me much. I think the guilt over his own behaviour sat too deep. But he told me how Marco had rejected you and kept you away from the family. That you grew up alone.'

An icy shiver clawed down her spine. That was a lot more than she usually told people. But Eliana found she didn't mind that Diego knew. With any other person the mortification would have been too much to cope with. But things were different with him. It was as if she wanted him to know.

'I can see he meant a great deal to you. No wonder you brought him here to meet your patchwork family.'

He'd not spoken about his half-siblings since they'd sat down. Now his gaze became distant as he looked up to the night sky.

'I like my siblings…even though I sometimes envy them for the relationships they've been able to build. While suffering the same father, at least they had their mothers to look out for them. My mother didn't care enough.' He heaved a drawn-out sigh. 'But Vanderson understood me like they never will.'

Diego envied his siblings? As she glimpsed more and more of the fragments of himself he hid behind those thick walls, she felt their connection solidify beyond the shared necessity of being parents together.

He understood her. He had made her the priority tonight and empowered her to make her own decisions. And he'd given her something of her brother she'd never thought she'd get.

'I wish I could've known him,' she said, and laid a hand on his thigh.

The small touch was enough to make him look up at her. 'Me too,' he replied, with a smile so sweet and full of longing it made her breath catch in her throat. 'He would have been excited about us. Shocked to his core, but also excited.'

'Since Vanderson was helping you, does that mean you now need *my* help to keep the clinic going?'

Diego's expression slipped for a second. A hopeful gleam entered his eyes, mixing with the intense fire she'd seen the moment he'd opened the door for her.

'That's not something I can ask of you. Not with everything between us being so...'

'Messy?' she asked when his voice trailed off.

'I would have phrased it with more delicacy if you'd given me a chance.' His voice was stern, but a smile was pulling at the corners of his lips when she glanced at him, chuckling herself.

'We'll find out soon enough when we need to compartmentalise work and parenting stuff. This can be our first test.' She paused, looking at him with intent. 'I think my father strayed very far from the path of putting patient care above anything else. If you tell me that Vanderson meant to change that, I'll want to continue on with that.'

She watched his entire demeanour change with each word she spoke, his posture relaxing and opening up, his expression one of such profound happiness and relief that Eliana almost gasped at the intense look he gave her. With a smile on his face, he wrapped his hands around her face and planted a short and hard kiss on her unprepared lips.

'I can't tell you how much this means to me— to my entire community. People like Miguel will be able to get the care they need when they need it.'

Shocked by the unexpected kiss—which she knew was a sign of gratitude and not of the burning desire she sensed coursing through her veins—she stared at him with a blank expression, blinking multiple times as she struggled to regain her composure.

Fires had erupted within her, starting in her core and spreading searing tendrils into every corner of her body. Their lips had touched for barely more than a second, but that was enough to thunder an almost impossible need for Diego through her.

His hands dropped from her face and he looked at her with wide eyes, seemingly surprised by his own action. 'I'm sorry... I shouldn't have,' he mumbled, although the narrowing of his eyes as his gaze darkened didn't show any of the regret he professed. Only the untamed hunger she'd seen in his face before.

It was a want that mirrored her own—and one that had led to the very reason they could never give in to one another. Not with a child involved between them. It would only lead to so much more heartbreak when they inevitably fell apart. Eliana wanted him. Everything deep inside her called out to him. But she needed safety more than anything else. Needed to matter to someone, to be their priority.

Though hadn't Diego shown her he'd made her exactly that today? Was it possible they could be something else even when they'd said they couldn't?

An awkward silence spread between them—the first one of the night—as they both grappled with their undeniable attraction to one another and their steadfast belief that they couldn't go there ever again.

Even though it kept happening.

'Have you told anyone yet?' he asked.

At his question Eliana looked down at her flat stomach, covering it with one hand and breathing a sigh of relief. The sooner they could move on from the tension brewing between them, the better.

'No one outside of the obstetrics department head. The first scan is soon.' She paused for a moment and looked up at him. A spark had entered his dark eyes, and his gaze was almost hypnotising her. 'Do you still want to come?'

'You want me there?' His voice was low, vibrating through her skin right into her core, raising the heat.

'You're the father—you have just as much right to be there as I have.'

'I'm not asking about my rights. Do you *want* me to be there?'

The tension between them came rushing back as he spoke those words, and she saw his eyes fill with an intent to conquer her.

'If you want to—'

'Ana.' He interrupted her, his voice low, filled with promises that made her heart beat fast against her chest. 'Do you want me?'

Eliana's mouth went dry and she swallowed. They had stopped talking about the scan. They were back to the tangible electricity filling her stomach with flutters. Did she want him? Want him how? At the scan? In her life? *Right now?*

What frightened her most was the fact that all those questions had the same answer.

'Yes,' she whispered, afraid that her voice would give out if she spoke too loudly, and watched him come closer...

The beast of unbridled desire within his chest had simply watched for most of the evening, rearing its head occasionally when he'd caught a glimpse of Eliana's smile or when her luscious scent had drifted up his nose.

From the moment she had walked through the door Diego had known that he would kiss her, that they would pick up where they had left off at the clinic. And this time he would make sure to follow through.

Kissing her in the back yard of his *avozinha*'s house had been a tactical error. He should have invited her to his place before drawing her into his arms. But he'd found himself unable to resist her any longer. Not after she'd said the one word he had been dying to hear from her lips.

Yes.

She wanted him. Just as much as he wanted her. That was all he needed to know to forget about where they were and who might potentially walk around the corner and catch them.

Eliana's warm breath trembled against his skin as he pulled her into his arms, his lips brushing against hers in a sensual invitation for her to get lost in the moment. It was an invitation she was clearly eager to receive, as she balled her hands around the fabric of his shirt and pulled him closer.

The passion swimming through his blood roared to life with that one kiss, sending heat cascading through his body. What was it about this woman that drove him over the edge with little more than a kiss? That made him keep coming back for more? That had allowed him to let his grandmother actually invite her to meet his family?

No woman ever got to meet any of the Ferrari clan.

Eliana opened her mouth and caught his lower lip between her teeth, giving it a short but intense squeeze that drew a groan of desire from his throat. She pulled back to look at him, an expression of want on her face. Her breath left her in an unsteady staccato, her chest heaving with anticipation.

Diego pulled her close again, deepening their kiss. This time Eliana let his tongue pass, moaning her mounting pleasure against his lips. His hands wandered over her back, finding the exposed flesh and brushing her with his fingertips. He remembered the softness of her skin beneath his hands that first night together, her taste as he'd explored her body at his leisure, drawing mewls of delight and release from her full lips.

How long had he been waiting for this to happen again? And how often had he told himself that he wasn't allowed to go there—ever? Only in this moment he couldn't remember why he'd been so against it. It was clear now that something special connected them—something that went beyond his understanding of relationships.

Was that why he always struggled to give in completely? Because he'd always be confronted by that crucial bit of information that he'd missed out on as a child? How to form a healthy and functioning relationship where both partners were equal. That wasn't what his parents had shown him.

This was lust burning in his chest—not some misguided emotional attachment. They had both said so themselves. Neither wanted a relationship that went beyond the way they would share custody of their child. If his parents had sought an arrangement the way he and Eliana were trying to right now, maybe things would have turned out differently. Maybe he would have known how to appreciate a tremendous woman like Eliana in more than one way.

His mouth left her lips, feathering light kisses down her neck and caressing her there. Need cascaded through him, reaching a boiling point when another enticing moan fell from her lips. They needed to go.

Diego brought a minimal amount of distance between them to look her in the eyes. They were smouldering with the same intensity he felt.

'My place is down the street,' he murmured, and excitement thundered through him when she grinned.

* * *

If it hadn't been for the fire in her core, Eliana might have forgotten why she was there when she entered Diego's house and took in the view. The hallway was almost as large as the hotel room she was staying in, with polished stone surfaces and tasteful decoration in the few places it was needed.

But Diego had other plans for her. The moment they got through the door he slammed it shut behind him and was upon her not even a heartbeat later, capturing her mouth with his.

He pressed her against the cold wall and she felt his fingers leaving exquisite fires as they roamed her body. She let her head fall backwards, surrendering her entire self to Diego and his caresses.

This wasn't supposed to happen… But the voice that kept on warning her about it—about their relationship getting too messy—was growing faint and easy to ignore.

What was the harm? As long as both of them remembered that she would soon be leaving and that they weren't looking for anything permanent, maybe they could loosen the leash on their desire for just one night. At least this time there wouldn't be any accidents.

His hands had found the zipper of her dress. With a twist of her shoulder he turned her around, and she pressed her front against the

wall while he pulled down the zipper with agonising slowness, leaving a scorching kiss every
time he uncovered more skin.

'*Deus*, Diego, *por favor...*' she whispered, as
unreserved need cascaded through her, bringing an intensity and wetness between her legs
that made her knees buckle.

'What do you want, *amor*?' His voice was
deep, filled with the restraint he was practising
by undressing her bit by bit, taking his sweet
time on this journey down her body.

'This is too much. I need you...*now.*'

The zipper stopped just above her bottom,
and Diego peeled the dress from her back, fold-
ing it over at the front before flipping her around
again. With one smooth motion he pulled on the
dress again, making it fall from her body and
pool around her feet.

The fire in his eyes made her breath catch
in her throat. This was different from what she
had seen in his face when they'd slept together
all those weeks ago. Something about this moment was different from before, and it made her
need for him burn all that brighter.

He kissed her, long and deep, tasting her
mouth as if he had never kissed her before. Her
thighs trembled when he pulled her against him,
and the full length of his erection was pressing
into her, urging.

'No,' he whispered when she slipped her

hands down to start removing his clothes. He took her wrist, wrapping his fingers around it. 'I want to be deliberate this time. I want to savour every moment, taste every part of you, until you have no more to give.'

'Diego…' Her breath came in bursts as his hands caressed her hips. He stopped for a moment when he stroked her stomach, drawing both of them back into the moment that had changed them for ever.

He glanced down, as if to check to see if he could find any trace of their child, and when his eyes came back to hers they were filled with a warmth that sent her pulse even higher.

'I was too focused on my own pleasure the first time around. I need to make it up to you,' he said close to her ear, raising the fine hair at the nape of her neck and on her arms.

Eliana looked at him for a moment, and in the next instant felt her feet leave the ground, making her yelp as she wrapped her hands around Diego's neck. He lifted her into his arms, carried her through the hall and down a corridor, into what she could only presume was his bedroom.

He let her drop on the bed, pouncing on her like a jaguar would jump on its prey, pinning her down. She shivered under the pressure of his body, writhing as his erection pushed against her again. It wasn't just her that wanted this. She was making him feel the same way, filling him with need and urgency. Eliana could see it in the tightness of his jaw as he lifted himself off her to trail gentle and warm kisses down her neck to her sternum, where he came to rest.

Eliana arched her back, pushing closer to him when his teeth gripped at the fabric of her bra, pulling the garment aside to expose her breasts to the cooling air of the Brazilian spring evening. The straps fell down from her shoulders as Diego found the clasp on the front, drawing the bra away from her body and throwing it on the floor.

Diego stopped for a moment, as if plotting his course, and a hungry growl was loosed from his throat. She propped herself up on her elbows, wanting to see what he was up to, but immediately fell back down with a long drawn-out moan when he sucked one of her peaked nipples into his mouth, rolling it around with his tongue.

A firework exploded in the pit of her stomach and her hips arched against his strong frame, as if begging to find any kind of release as the lines between pleasure and pain began to blur.

'Diego…' she whispered, unable to form any other coherent words, trusting that her voice would carry enough meaning for him to understand.

Please, don't stop.

He didn't.

His mouth left one breast to go to the other, lavishing it with the same attention and pleasure he had given the first one, before moving on down over her stomach, his lips and tongue leaving featherlight traces on her skin as if he was mapping her body so he could remember every detail.

Wasn't that what he'd said? That he wanted to remember everything about this moment? Eliana had thought it no more than a line from a man who had seen many women before her and would see many after her, too. But that was not how he made her feel in this moment—as if he was a trained lover going through the steps he had taken many times before. No, to her it seemed all of his attention was focused on her and on what made her writhe in pleasure. That thought alone was enough to renew the need inside her that settled into the wetness at her core.

What made this moment different from that night two months ago? It couldn't be that it was simply because they had started to get to know each other. To build a tentative friendship upon which they wanted to build the foundation of their co-parenting adventure. Was that enough to have such an impact?

Her thoughts were catapulted back into the present when the silk of her underwear scraped against her thighs as Diego moved them down in one smooth motion of his arm. His fingers brushed over her mound as he lowered his face to kiss her thighs, each time slipping just a bit further up, until she felt his breath right next to the place his hand had been caressing.

Her anticipation of what was going to happen next transformed into an eruption of untold pleasure when Diego parted her with one stroke of his tongue and lavished her with its attention.

Eliana fisted one hand into the linen underneath her as a trembling shook her body, and the beginning of a climax was already building inside her as her breath left her mouth in ragged bursts, mingling with the moans he coaxed out of her. Her other hand found Diego's as he caressed her stomach, and she gripped him as if she was holding on for dear life.

'Please, don't stop.'

This time she managed to articulate the words as the waves of her climax started to build, crashing through her with a ferocity that wiped any thought from her brain.

Diego's name clung to her lips as she gave in, losing herself in the pleasure that rocked through her. The muscles in her thighs tensed for a moment before they relaxed again, her breath still unsteady and coming out in bursts.

She felt him smile against her thighs as he kissed one and then the other, trailing small kisses up her stomach until he was on top of her, looking into her eyes with an intensity that brought a new surge of need to her core just as the first one was receding.

Eliana opened her mouth, wanting to say something, though she wasn't sure what. But he stopped her, laying a gentle finger on her mouth, tracing her lower lip before bending down and kissing her. Her mouth was filled with his taste, the warmth of his tongue, and she gripped at his shoulders so as to not drift away in the luscious cloud of ecstasy he had conjured around them.

'You are incredible, you know that?' he whispered against her neck, before his mouth trailed down again and goosebumps made all the little hairs rise on her body.

Her expression had changed for a fraction of a second, doubt clouding her eyes. Diego halted, looking at her intently, keen to know her thoughts. But before he could say anything her hands had found their way past his waistband. His button popped open with one flick of her finger, and one of her hands pulled at his T-shirt while the other wrapped itself around his shaft, stroking...

A low growl escaped his lips—a lot more feral than he'd intended to be. The moment he had seen the dress drop from her shoulders, exposing her incredible strength and a grace that shone from inside out, Diego had known he wanted to worship her all night. And that even then he wouldn't be worthy of a woman like Eliana. She had endured so much loss and rejection in her life, but instead of letting that experience harden her heart she had emerged from the pain with a softness and a kindness that brought him to his knees.

But now he was enjoying a glimpse of the other Eliana. The one he had met at the bar. Who knew exactly what she wanted and wasn't afraid to take matters into her own hands.

And what incredibly skilled hands she had.

Diego groaned again as she pulled his trousers down, and hardly noticed when she pulled his shirt over his head and threw it onto the pile of clothes already on the floor.

'Hang on,' he said, when Eliana hooked her leg around his waist and flipped their bodies so that he was lying on his back.

A wicked grin appeared on her face as she sat on top of him, his taut length straining against her. 'No. We've done it your way. Now we do it my way, Ferrari,' she replied.

And Diego closed his eyes with a primal moan when she released the tension in her thighs and let him sink into her in his entirety.

Her nails scratched along his bare chest as they moved their hips in harmony, and Eliana's small cries of pleasure were already threatening to undo him when he wanted this moment to last for ever.

Because this moment was perfection. They were permitted to be who they were—two people attracted to each other, who were finding their path towards their true feelings for each other. As long as they remained like this, they were allowed to be these two people.

The moment they finished Diego knew the spell the evening had woven around them would break, leaving them to cope with the reality of their lives. With the fact that they were not built for the type of relationships others had. Not after everything that had happened to them.

But right now he just wanted to feel this incredible woman crushed against his body as they lost themselves in their burning passion for one another.

With another groan, Diego pulled his upper body off the bed, slinging his arms around her torso and hugging her close to his chest before turning them around once more so he was on top of her.

'Ana, I—' He interrupted himself, pressing his mouth on hers again, wrapping her in an indulgent kiss as he sensed their shared climax approaching.

And with that kiss full of promise and tenderness he felt the release wash over him, as Eliana, too, cried out his name, writhing underneath him with a sob of pleasure.

CHAPTER EIGHT

THE GENTLE BRUSH of fingers against her exposed back coaxed Eliana out of her slumber. She felt warm breath on the back of her neck, and she stretched her legs and toes as she enjoyed Diego's caress.

'Bom dia, meu amor,' he whispered near her ear, and sent sparks flying down her spine.

'You shouldn't call me that,' she mumbled back, but instead of pulling away she snuggled closer into his hard and warm chest.

My love. Such an endearment was way too intimate for what they were…which was something they hadn't defined. She had spent every night of the last week at Diego's, entangled in his sheets most of the time, but also talking with him about anything they could come up with.

Now he didn't reply, instead nuzzling into her neck, the kisses he traced on her skin making her shiver with renewed need.

'Don't you need to be somewhere? I'm sure

I told Suelen to make sure your surgical schedule is full.'

Through the thick fog of desire, Eliana grasped at straws. Anything to make him move away, even though that was the last thing she wanted him to do. And he knew she didn't really want him to go.

Diego chuckled into her hair, pulling her even closer to his chest. 'It's Sunday. We don't have to be anywhere if we don't want to.'

No, don't say that.

She needed him to be busy so she could find enough distance to get away. To think. Right now, all her emotions were tangled up in the visceral and deep connection they shared on more than just a physical level. While the sex was mind-bending, Eliana could see a pattern beneath it. There was a reason for it, and it had precious little to do with skill and everything with how she felt. For him, in particular.

And she must not feel anything for him. That wasn't part of the plan. The plan was to find an easy-going friendship so they could make decisions about their baby together.

As if he had read her mind, Diego slipped a hand down to her naked stomach, gently resting his palm on the smallest of bumps that was forming where their child was growing. It was that little bump that she should remember whenever her feelings for him were getting messy and tangled. Her baby deserved a stable home, even if it was only with one parent.

'You haven't felt anything yet, have you?' he asked.

Eliana shook her head and laid her hand on top of his. 'No, it's too early at the end of the first trimester. But at least I'm done with morning sickness.'

He hummed low, the vibration seeping through her pores and into her body, awakening a new wave of want for this man.

'I'm going to have to tell Avozinha. She'll be thrilled, and probably won't leave you alone once she knows.'

Diego had meant it as a jovial threat, but she actually found herself excited at the prospect of someone else partaking in the joy she had so far kept to herself. Even though everything leading up to her baby's conception had been an accident—and the situation with her Dr Dad was not in the least bit clear—she was genuinely excited to meet her child, and had felt sad that no one would be there to share that happiness with her.

Except now there was Diego, his *avozinha* and, by extension, the entire Ferrari clan. Her child would be able to know its extended family—people who cared about knowing their new niece, cousin or great-granddaughter. Despite Diego's claim that he wasn't close to his siblings, she could see they genuinely cared about one another. And now about her, too.

'Márcia was the one who raised you?' she asked.

Behind her, Diego stiffened for a moment, his lips still touching her skin. He relaxed after a few heartbeats, mumbling his response into her hair.

'She did. After one of my parents' countless breakups and subsequent reconciliations, they wanted to bring me back home after I'd spent several months with my grandmother. She refused to hand me over and instead told them to come back if they managed to go a whole year without splitting up again.' He let out a humourless chuckle. 'They didn't last half as long. So my *avozinha* ended up raising me and made sure to involve herself with my half-siblings too, so I could get to know them. It's thanks to her that I turned out the way I did.'

'You can tell her if you want,' Eliana said, wriggling around in his arms so she could look at him.

'Are you sure? She'll probably start making baby clothes straight away and drop them off at the hospital.'

She laughed at the thought of her office being transformed into a nursery. 'Maybe wait until I'm back in Belo Horizonte. Save the new chief the madness of finding baby sleepsuits in every drawer.'

They chuckled together, though this time she thought there was a strange sense of loss mixed into their laughter. Her departure was looming, and would take her an eight-hour drive away from Rio de Janeiro. She would leave soon, and they hadn't got any closer to understanding how they would work together as parents. Were they trying to put the cart in front of the horse? Was that why it was so difficult even to talk about it? And she knew a part of her yearned to stay here so her child could be close to its family.

'When are you leaving?' He tried to sound casual, but she sensed the tension in his muscles.

She shrugged. 'Soon. I've made my choice as Chief of Medicine, we're just finalising the handover, and then I'll have no more reason to stay here.'

Except you.

The words echoed in her mind, daring her to speak them, but they turned to bitter ash as she swallowed them. She couldn't let herself go there—not with all the mess around them. Diego was a man of enormous calibre and skill, and his compassion for his community ran so deep Eliana could only hope to feel so strongly one day.

But, especially after last night, she knew she

could never be a part of his world. Despite all the adversity he had witnessed as a child, he had managed to find his family, bond with them in a significant way that she never would.

Having grown up isolated from everyone around her, Eliana didn't know how to be a part of a family and doubted she could ever learn. Watching the Ferrari siblings interact with another had filled her with a yearning so deep, and it had hurt to know she would never have what they had.

'Who did you pick?' Diego asked, interrupting her thoughts mid-stream.

'Sophia.'

He arched his eyebrows in a surprised look. 'Sophia Salvador? The head of A&E? That's… actually a really good choice.'

'I spent so much time agonising over this decision, so your approval means a lot.'

Diego shot her a grin that made her heart skip a beat. She felt the heat rushing back to her core.

'Why was it a hard decision?' he asked.

'Because the hospital is infested with my father's people, who would be perfectly happy to stay the course it's on when what Santa Valeria really needs is a change for the better,' Eliana scoffed. 'The hospital should be known for the incredible talent of its medical staff—not for how nice the en-suite bathrooms of the patients' rooms are.'

She had made that exact speech in front of the board of directors as well, though they hadn't been impressed.

To her surprise, Diego laughed. 'You would get along well with Alessandro, Vanderson's husband. Vanderson could be a bit timid around his father, not wanting to draw too much attention to himself. Alessandro had no such reservations.'

'I would love to meet him,' she whispered.

She had only learned about him last week. With Vanderson's death, she'd believed her only link to her family was dead too, until Diego had dropped the bombshell around her brother-in-law and her niece.

Her child's cousin...

'You would?' There was an edge of surprise to his voice. 'I can take you to his shop. Daria might even be there, since it's the weekend.'

Her pulse quickened and her mouth went dry. She'd meant that wish to be a quiet desire, but had blurted it out before she'd been able to stop herself—something that seemed to happen way too often around Diego and his disarming smile.

Meeting her brother-in-law? The thought both terrified and excited her. But after seeing the dynamic between Diego and his siblings she wanted to see whether her child could have something like that as well—even if it was with a cousin rather than a sibling.

'I would like that.'

By the time they arrived at the Copa Cabana, where Alessandro ran his store, Eliana was a puddle of nerves, and Diego was fighting the need to chuckle by biting the inside of his cheek. Normally so confident and sure of herself, she seemed to be struggling with the thought of meeting a family member she hadn't known she had.

Although if he put it in those words, he could understand why she felt nervous. Diego himself had met so many mystery half-siblings and cousins he had never previously heard of that the situation bothered him very little—which was probably more a statement about his father's promiscuity than anything else.

They stood on the beach, a few paces away from Alessandro's store. A small café was attached to it, with some tables sprawled around the entrance. Behind the store was a five-metre-high climbing wall that made Diego smile when he looked at it.

When he'd been a more frequent visitor here, he'd sometimes do his workout by climbing that wall. Daria had often egged him on, asking him to climb faster and higher.

As if his thoughts had summoned her, a small

girl burst through the doors of the shop and bolted towards the pair. Diego smiled, going down on one knee so the girl could run straight into his arms.

'Tio! Where have you been? You said you would visit more often.'

Daria launched into a flood of sentences that he barely understood as they hugged each other, and he felt a twinge of guilt in his chest. He had only come to visit them once since the funeral.

'I'm sorry, *meu anjo*. You know how I get busy with work sometimes.'

Daria nodded gravely, as if she knew exactly how difficult the life of a surgeon was. Then she noticed Eliana, who now stood next to him.

'Daria, this is my friend Ana,' he said, and closed the gap between him and Eliana. 'Where is your *papai*?'

'Never too far away when she runs out of the store,' a low male voice said.

Diego set Daria down. She ran over to her father as he got closer to her. Alessandro came to a halt a couple of paces away from them but didn't even look at Diego. His eyes went straight to Eliana, and from the surprised and pained expression on his face it was clear that he had immediately spotted the similarities between her and Vanderson that Diego himself had missed that fateful night at the hotel.

'You're…his sister?' he asked, and Eliana nodded.

Tears sparkled in their eyes as they fell into each other's arms in an emotional display that robbed Diego of any remaining air in his lungs. He had thought that meeting Alessandro might be important to Eliana, but he had never imagined how emotional it would be for everyone— him included.

'Do you have time to sit down for a bit?' asked Alessandro, and Eliana looked over her shoulder to Diego, who shrugged.

He ushered them to one of the café's tables, where they sat down together, quiet for a moment.

'You could have given me a warning,' Alessandro said as he crossed his arms in front of his chest. 'You know I hate surprises.'

Diego smirked. 'That's why I didn't tell you.'

The man scowled at him, but his expression immediately softened when he looked over to Eliana. 'You really shouldn't put up with him… he's bad news.'

'Well…' She hesitated, her hand slipping to her stomach as she looked at Diego with a silent question: *Should we tell him?*

It was something Diego had thought about since he'd found out about her pregnancy. Eventually he'd need to tell the people around him that he was going to be a father. But their journey had been such an unconventional one he didn't know how to start explaining that he was having a child when he hadn't been in a relationship with a woman...ever.

Once someone outside of the two of them knew about the baby it would change everything. But Alessandro and Daria were the only people she had left that resembled her family; it was only natural that she wanted to connect with them by sharing their news.

Were they ready for that step?

There was only one way to find out.

Diego took a breath and gave her a small nod, which she acknowledged with a smile. Was she excited to be telling them?

'I know I've only just met you, so this may sound a bit strange. But Diego and I are actually having a child.'

Alessandro's eyes went wide with surprise, and his gaze darted between them as if he couldn't understand what she had just said. 'You two are...?'

'We're not together, no! This is an accident. We met some months ago now.'

She'd voiced her denial so rapidly it took Diego a few moments to register the hurt blooming in his chest. Which was ridiculous, since he *knew* they weren't together. He had set that expectation from the very beginning, so it shouldn't surprise him that she believed him.

Had *his* feelings changed?

They couldn't have. He didn't know how to love with every fibre of his being. Didn't know how to behave in the kind of family he secretly wanted to have. Alessandro and Vanderson had been the role models for something he knew he would never be able to achieve, no matter how much he desired it. So he had contented himself with watching from the side lines as their family came together and grew.

Being a minor character in their story was better than becoming a tragic failure in his own, right?

Except now here they sat, their roles reversed. He had made a child with this woman next to him, who had endured so much injustice and loneliness without letting it affect her heart.

She always tried to appear strong and independent when people were paying attention— a reflex no doubt born from the neglect she'd experienced during her childhood years. But whenever she thought no one was looking the guards came down and she became a much softer person. A person who would call their unborn child 'princess' because she felt a connection strong enough to know with certainty it was a girl.

He'd seen the same woman this last week as their passion had been transformed into something much more profound right in front of his eyes. He'd seen her come apart and put herself back together right under his hands, heard her whisper his name in the dead of the night as he pulled her closer into his embrace.

Everything in those moments had made sense in a way he hadn't experienced before. It had all just felt right, suddenly, and he felt like a fool for ever believing he couldn't have what he'd sensed last night. What he felt right now in this moment, as they told the first other person that they were having a child together.

Only she had rejected all those feelings with one phrase.

'I can't believe it. Of all the men you could have found in Rio, you've tied yourself to the eternal bachelor. That's material for a telenovela right there.' Alessandro looked at Diego. 'How do you feel?'

As if his world was falling apart right underneath his feet. Everything he'd thought to be true about himself had shifted since he'd met Eliana, and now he couldn't go on without her—didn't want to know what it felt like to be without her. She had found the thing Diego had thought he was missing. It had been inside him all this time, waiting for the right person to find it. Waiting for her.

'Better than you give me credit for,' he said, to distract himself from his own inner turmoil. 'I have you to show me how to be a good father.'

Alessandro laughed at that and looked down at Daria, who was sitting on a chair next to him and was busy enjoying her milkshake. She stopped drinking when she noticed her father looking at her and tilted her head, clearly oblivious to the discussion that had gone on between the adults.

'I think you're not giving yourself enough credit for turning out to be a decent man despite all the obstacles,' Alessandro said with a pointed look. 'I can think of a lot of different reactions to an unplanned pregnancy.'

Diego glanced at Eliana, who had gone quiet during their exchange, her hand still resting on the tiny bump that was starting to form.

'It wasn't how I planned to have a child, but I'm glad it happened the way it did,' she said. 'Diego hasn't shied away from taking responsibility. We're just trying to figure things out as we go along, while I'm still wrapping up things with Marco's estate.'

There was a softness in her words that caught Diego off guard. Was it affection? After she had rejected him so resoundingly he hadn't expected to encounter such warmth only a few moments later. Was she *glad* they'd had an accident on their first night together? That it had been with Diego?

'I mean, how else would I have met you?' she added, looking at Alessandro with a wide smile.

Their connection had been instantaneous, and Diego was happy for her. After the way Marco had isolated his own daughter from any kind of family life, she deserved to know some of her roots.

She halted for a moment, her eyes trailing over to the sea for a moment. 'I didn't see your name on any of the papers in my father's will. Vanderson was his only beneficiary, but after the accident…'

Alessandro shook his head with a sad smile. 'You're sweet to worry. But Vanderson had his own estate and that went to us as his next of kin. Me not getting along with Marco didn't affect us as a family.' Alessandro smiled, reaching over the table to grab Eliana's hand and squeeze it. 'Make sure Diego gives you my number so we can keep in touch. Daria will be thrilled to meet her little cousin in a few months. Isn't that right, *anjinho*?'

Daria beamed at all of them and nodded. Her excitement to meet her new cousin was palpable in her face. Diego heard a soft gasp coming from Eliana, and saw the shimmer covering her eyes as she looked at her niece with a big smile.

'I can't wait for you all to meet this little one.'

A noisy group of tourists walking towards the shop interrupted their discussion, and Alessandro stood up with a sigh.

'I have to take care of this.' He walked over to Eliana and pulled her into another hug. 'Let's grab some coffee when it's less busy, so we can have a chance to chat. I'm sure there are a lot of things you would like to know about Vanderson, and it would be nice to relive the memories I have of him.'

She nodded in agreement before hugging Daria as well and waving as they both scurried back into the store. When she sat down again, her face was unreadable.

'How are you feeling? Lots to process?' Diego asked, and looked at her for a moment before laying a hand on her thigh to give it a supportive squeeze.

'I like him. It's good to know that at least Vanderson had the chance at a normal life. Although no doubt my father left a lot of damage on him as well.'

At least. The words hung between them like a dark fog, suddenly rushing in to envelop everything around them. It sounded as if she had given up.

An invisible band had been constricting his chest since she'd spoken those words about her pregnancy, and he had now got to a point where his chest felt heavy under the crushing sensation. He couldn't hide his mounting feelings for Eliana any longer and had to admit to himself that he wanted more from her. More than he had ever wanted from anyone before and more than she was willing to give.

Which left him with no choice but to forget about how he felt. How he had fallen so hard without even noticing? She didn't want him the way he wanted her, and maybe that was for the best. How could he promise her a happy family when he had no idea how to make one? Better to make the best out of what they already had rather than try for something new.

'What do you want to do now?' he asked. 'The climbing wall is a lot of fun if you're feeling brave.'

She laughed. 'Making a baby from scratch has left me a bit exhausted, so I'll pass on the extreme sports for now. How about a walk on the beach instead?'

He smiled as he took her hand, their fingers weaving into each other's as they started their stroll, and a warmth rising in his arms from where their skin connected.

She would leave any day now. Eliana had said so herself. And Diego was determined to enjoy the time they had left, even if he was dreaming of what might have been if they had grown up differently.

The water sparkled in the light of the afternoon sun as they walked down the beach in a comfortable silence. The meeting with Alessandro had healed a part of Eliana's heart in a way only he could have done. With him she had regained a connection to her brother, and even though he wasn't here to explain, she was glad to know someone who could tell her who he had been besides what Diego had already told her.

Diego's support had been essential in this endeavour. It showed her he cared not just for his child but for her. Getting to know Alessandro—that would be for her alone.

She felt her already bleeding heart squeeze even tighter. Diego's affection meant so much to her when it really shouldn't. At some point would she have to admit that they might have gone too deep?

Eliana shook those thoughts away, instead focusing on the beach around her and the warmth his hand created where it touched hers, radiating heat through her entire body. It might be the last time she got to enjoy such a tranquil moment before she left Rio behind.

'Have you been here before?' Diego asked as they stopped to watch two people zip past them on a pair of quad bikes with frightening speed.

'Not really.' Her eyes followed the bikes as they wove through people. She heard excited laughter trailing after the drivers. 'I didn't like going out by myself when I lived here, and by the time I was older I had already moved away.'

'You haven't missed much. The Copa Cabana

gets so many reviews online every visitor comes here.' The bikes came zooming around again and he raised his hand, underlining the point he'd just made. 'I know a private beach that I—'

A loud bang drowned out the rest of his sentence and Eliana clasped her hand over her mouth as one of the quad bikes collided with a palm tree, sending the rider flying over the steering wheel and into the trunk before he fell on the ground unmoving.

Diego swore next to her and sprinted towards the person lying in the sand. She quickly followed him, scanning the people who were moving closer. When she spotted someone holding a phone, she pointed at them.

'Please call for an ambulance and say to the operator that there has been a motor vehicle crash on the beach.' Eliana didn't wait for a reply but turned around to find Diego kneeling beside the man, who had regained consciousness and was moaning in agony.

'What's the status? Anything I can do to help?'

Both the man's arms stood at unnatural angles. One had a dislocated shoulder, the other a potential fracture of the lower arm. A quick glance showed her the skin was still intact, though that didn't mean the breaking bone hadn't done some damage to the muscles and blood vessels in the arm.

Diego looked at his patient, assessing the damage before bending over the man again. '*Senhor*, do you hear me?' he asked, and the man nodded with a wince. 'We are both doctors and we're here to help. You've had an accident and crashed.'

Eliana knelt down as well, waiting for Diego's plan of action. Whatever the man's wounds were, she knew he'd been lucky that Diego was here to help with stabilising the fracture.

A small part inside her felt excited to be working with him. As chief at the hospital she'd spoken to many people working with Diego, and none of the other department heads had received such high praise. The compassion and care he gave each patient, no matter the severity of the case, was unparalleled, and after seeing for herself his interaction with Miguel, as well as the man in front of him now, she could see his staff had not exaggerated.

'We can't set the bone without an X-ray, but we can pop the shoulder back in and stabilise the arm with a sling until the ambulance arrives,' Diego said to her before turning back to the patient.

'Is he going to be okay?' His friend had stopped her bike a few paces away and now came running over.

Diego stood up for a moment, laying a hand on her shoulder. 'We have to get him to a hospital, but he is conscious. What I'm about to do will hurt without anaesthesia. Can you sit next to him?'

She nodded, her face as pale as the sand surrounding them, and dropped to her knees beside him.

'Have you relocated a shoulder before?' Diego asked Eliana as he came down next to the patient's head.

'I've watched several, but never done it myself.'

'Can you kneel behind his back once we prop him up? This will be rough on him, but it'll make things a lot easier for the ambulance.'

When Eliana nodded, he pushed the man's torso off the ground and she settled behind him, holding him upright while Diego took the arm with the dislocated shoulder between his hands.

'Most of the time you'll find that the tendons in the arm help the shoulder find its way back. All you have to do is pull.'

Eliana watched as he tightened his grip around the man's arm and pulled at it with a sharp but precise motion that sent a tremble through the patient's body accompanied by a stifled shout.

'Then follow the pressure of the tendons to bring the shoulder back into its socket.'

He got to his feet, asking one of the onlookers if he could borrow her towel and fashioning it into a makeshift sling, into which he carefully lifted the broken arm to stabilise it for transport.

'I know you're in a lot of pain right now, and the last thing you want is some doctor asking you questions,' he said, in a soothing voice that even managed to set Eliana at ease. 'But I have to ask one so we can make sure we're not missing anything. Are you feeling any nausea or sickness?'

The man's chest fluttered with each laboured breath, but he shook his head from one side to the other.

'We can't rule out a concussion, but at least he was wearing a helmet,' Eliana said, and Diego nodded.

His hand slipped inside his pocket, fishing out his smartphone. He turned the torch on with a flick of his finger, shining the light into the patient's eyes. 'Pupillary reaction looks good. Fingers crossed we have no spinal or head injuries.'

They both looked up when the sirens of an ambulance came closer and a red and white vehicle came into view. Two paramedics came running, with a gurney in their hands.

Eliana watched as Diego updated them on the patient's status and then took a step back as they readied him for transportation to the nearest emergency department. Her eyes flickered between the patient and Diego, who was now talking to the patient's friend.

'They're taking him to Copa Memorial for treatment. The ambulance can take you along if you want to accompany them.'

The woman's eyes were shining with tears at this point, and she looked around to the bikes. 'I want to, but…'

Diego followed her gaze. 'Did you rent them from the store with the climbing wall behind it?' He smiled when she nodded. 'The owner happens to be a good friend of mine, so don't worry about it. We'll sort it out. Go with him.'

The woman thanked them both with a sob in her voice and they watched her climb into the ambulance.

'You were incredible,' Eliana said, giving voice to the brewing thought within her. Not only had he kept the patient calm under chaotic circumstances, he'd been able to help with very limited resources.

Diego looked at her in surprise. 'I don't think so…'

Eliana laughed at the denial. 'I'm glad I got to watch you work before I leave. Now I know why your staff keep saying such nice things about you. Santa Valeria is lucky to have you to teach its staff the right way.'

He crossed his arms in front of his chest,

raising his eyebrows. 'Did the doctors in your hospital never help in emergencies?'

'Of course they did. What I'm trying to say is that I love your compassion and your dedication to doing the right thing. And after speaking to everyone at Santa Valeria I know that more people who think and act like you are needed.'

His brown eyes grew darker, narrowing on her and sending a shiver crawling down her spine. There was an unspoken desire written in them, something neither of them wanted to acknowledge. Speaking of it would undermine every boundary they had established between them—every agreement they had made for the good of their baby.

So Eliana bit her lip, swallowing the words rising in her throat, and looked at the quad bikes instead.

'Let's get these bikes back to Alessandro,' she said, needing to break the sudden intensity between them.

CHAPTER NINE

THE MORNING LIGHT filtering through the half-drawn curtains fell onto Eliana's face. She tried to turn around but met surprising resistance in the form of Diego, who had his arms wrapped around her waist and was pulling her into him even as he slept.

She looked down at herself. Her naked body was wrapped up in his sheets, her bare back hot where it connected with his chest. Their one night together, which should have been a one-off lapse of judgement, had extended into the last three weeks, with them spending both days and nights together.

The way they had been living was so far removed from what their lives would look like once she left—which would be soon. And they were nowhere near figuring out the arrangements for their co-parenting journey. Instead of focusing on that, they had given in to the tension that had been building between them for weeks.

Misguided tension.

Nothing about their situation had changed. Eliana was still going to leave, handing the hospital over so she didn't have to be involved any more. The city reminded her too much of Marco and what he had done to her. And although spending time with Diego opened her heart in ways she had never experienced before, there was still a sneaky voice in her head, whispering words of caution and poisoning these moments they were sharing together.

He'd shown incredible kindness and dedication to his community. But she'd also glimpsed the ruthlessness with which he had gone about it—taking resources from the hospital as well as smuggling people in. Diego had always acted for the right reasons and was ready to put his own career on the line for it, but would he do the same for her? Would he consider her part of his people when her struggle had been so different?

The doubts gnawing at her heart with their sharp claws and teeth did little to help her relax back into slumber. Every time she closed her eyes her thoughts started to whirl around in her head, corrupting what had been three weeks full of pleasure, laughter and closeness.

With a soft sigh on her lips Eliana turned around—and gasped when she stared right into Diego's warm brown eyes.

'Good morning,' she said, when his eyes narrowed as if he had caught every thought that had just wandered through her head.

'Do you want me to let you go?' he asked in a calm voice, and Eliana got the impression that he wasn't necessarily talking about his arms around her waist.

She took a breath to steady herself. His gaze was throwing her off balance, to the point where she couldn't quite remember exactly what she had been afraid of.

'I have to go to the hospital. My first scan is later today, and I need to get some things done before that,' she said, to wriggle out of telling him about her thoughts. 'As a matter of fact, you need to be in the hospital, too. The mayor's wife is getting her hip replaced today, and she's insisted she will only have the best surgeon touch her.'

Diego groaned, but the sound was very unlike the sounds that had filled her ears throughout the night as he came back for more of her.

'It's a hip replacement. Any second-year registrar can do that. You're just wasting money, putting the head of orthopaedics on this.' He sighed and released his grip around her to scrub his hands across his face. 'That money would be better spent on something ground-breaking—like fixing curved spines. A doctor from Peru has contacted me about a patient who has a fifty-degree bend they can't fix with steel rods.'

Eliana took the opportunity to roll out of bed, stepping out of Diego's range so he couldn't grab her again. 'Write down a proposal and we can talk about your curved spine. But until then I expect you to give the mayor's wife the very best care. From what the accountants tell me, she's a huge benefactor of the hospital.'

Eliana bent down to pick up her clothes, and when she looked back up Diego's face had changed. The humour in his eyes had died, leaving nothing but an icy tundra where she had just seen warmth and compassion.

'Don't tell me you're putting people with deep pockets ahead of patients who actually need help?'

The accusation came out of nowhere, and Eliana's chest constricted for a moment. She was surprised by the ferocity with which he'd spat those words at her.

'You know I'm not. But big donors are part of the ecosystem, too.'

Diego snorted in derision. 'That phrase comes straight out of Marco Costa's playbook.'

The ice in his gaze took over her body, trickling down her spine and through her body as if someone had poured cold water all over her.

'Do not compare me to that man,' she said, fighting to keep her voice even. 'You don't know what he was like as a person. You only ever interacted with him when you were trying to bend the rules in your favour. Any chief would be annoyed with you over that.'

Her chest heaved as she stared at him, looking for the man she had got to know so much about in the last few weeks, believing she might be able to trust him with the thoughts dwelling inside her. But his expression was unreadable.

'The same goes for you,' he said. 'If you're suddenly so concerned with profits I might have made a mistake showing you my clinic.'

His voice had dropped low, but instead of it causing the usual goosebumps of pleasure to coat her skin she felt the hairs on her arms stand on end in warning.

'Where do you think the money for expensive Peruvian surgeries comes from? All this because you think yourself too good to do a hip replacement?'

Eliana stared at him, waiting for a reply that didn't come. How could Diego accuse her of being like her father when she had worked so hard to support his vision of Santa Valeria's future?

'I don't want to waste my time appeasing rich people when there are others who need my help,' he said, with such quiet fury that Eliana glared at him.

Sprawled out in the bed like that, he would have been a breathtaking picture of masculine sensuality if she'd been able to see past his almost irrational response to one surgery. It wasn't as if she'd cancelled his entire surgical schedule and asked him to focus only on the mayor's wife.

'You are helping the hospital by doing this. The hospital you have, in essence, been *stealing* from for the last few years.'

He sat up, opening his mouth to speak, but she stopped him with a shake of her head. She knew she would regret letting this conversation go any further than she already had.

'I'm going to leave and let you contemplate who you just compared me to.' She paused for a moment; her hands balled into tight fists at her sides as she sensed the anger rising in her. 'I have the scan today, at two in the afternoon. It's at the hospital, so I'll see you there.'

Despite feeling wholly justified to uninvite him, she realised she needed to be the bigger person. He was still the father of her child.

Without giving him a chance to rope her into any further argument, Eliana took her clothes and fled the room, getting dressed in a hurry before leaving the house with tears of deep hurt stinging her eyes.

'You're an idiot.'

Diego looked up when the voice of his sister Gloria ripped him out of his contemplations.

He had been ready to leave for the hospital when his *avozinha* had called, asking if he could take her along. Miguel had just received his new leg, and she wanted to pay him and his mother a visit.

In typical Márcia fashion, she had been nowhere near ready when her grandson had pulled over to pick her up. So he had come inside to make himself some coffee as he waited. He'd need a lot of caffeine if he wanted to get through the day in one piece.

'Good morning to you, too,' he said, in a low voice that conveyed his overall annoyance with the way his day had started.

'I can't believe you finally bring home a woman and then you mess it up within a month.' She paused to look at him.

'How could you possibly know about that?' The accuracy with which Gloria had pinpointed the source of his annoyance was bordering on spooky.

'You were happy when we last saw you. Not just content, but actually smiling and engaging. None of us had ever seen you that way, so it was easy to guess what was different since you did us the favour of bringing her here.'

Diego crossed his arms, narrowing his eyes at his sister. 'Did you call the council of siblings to discuss this?'

Gloria chuckled—which didn't help his sour

mood. He didn't need anyone butting into his affairs.

'No, Albert saw you two interlocked. He said it looked like you were eating something off her neck.'

Diego glared at her, the exasperation in his chest fading away as he was confronted with the truth he'd been struggling with. He wanted to pretend that Eliana's exit that morning didn't mean anything to him.

'Our nephew saw us?' he asked.

Gloria nodded and couldn't hide her grin. 'You made out with someone in Avozinha's garden while the whole family was here. You couldn't have done a better job if you'd wanted to be caught.'

He hadn't thought about being caught when he had kissed Eliana in the garden. That moment had been about releasing something that had been dwelling inside him ever since they'd met during that surgery. Just moments before they had heard that they were having a child together for the first time. Such news should have made him wary of the woman involved, but instead they had grown closer.

'I'm still waiting to know why I'm the idiot here.' He cast a suspicious glance at his sister, who shook her head with a click of her tongue, as if the answer was the most obvious in the world.

'Because I was out walking Pelé when I saw Eliana leave your place in what looked like a hurry. Now, a woman you take to meet your ridiculous family must be special, because in all the years of our urging you to bring someone the best you could do was Vanderson. And no one ever caught you two making out.'

Diego grimaced, his thoughts still catching up with what Gloria had just revealed. The night at his grandmother's house had not gone as he had planned—which might be something of an overstatement. There hadn't been much planning going on after he'd kissed her. All he'd known was that he had to have her in his house. Not just to sleep with her, but to watch her fall asleep. To have her warm body next to him while he drifted off.

In a completely uncharacteristic move, Diego had found himself yearning for more than just a physical connection. And throughout their nights together, he had started to think about their future—if there could even be a future for them together. He had been close to talking to her about it, to discussing with her the blooming feelings in his chest that he had never felt before.

Until Eliana had mentioned his scheduled procedure on the mayor's wife and a wave of deep-seated anger had come rushing into his chest, banishing any other emotion that might have been there for the duration of a few heart-beats. Marco had done that sort of thing—constantly cancelling essential or even urgent surgeries so he could do a routine procedure that any registrar could handle on people who were important and brought in significant donations. They had been put ahead of people with genuine needs who needed his steady hands and exceptional skill to help them.

It wasn't a trend Diego wanted to see continue under the new leadership, so when she had mentioned it something inside him had snapped.

He'd stared at the ceiling after she'd left, his rage subsiding with each breath and being replaced with a feeling of profound unease.

His words had hurt her, and he had meant them to have that effect, but as he'd lain there regret had crept in. The hospital needed big donors to keep going—he understood that well enough. And none of his urgent patients had been bumped further down the line for him to do this procedure. Had his anger been an over-reaction because of the issues he'd experienced in the past?

'She's pregnant, Gloria,' he said now, letting go of the weight he'd been carrying around. 'We're having a child.'

Her eyebrows shot up. 'Then you'd better get your act together, big brother.'

A thought occurred to Diego that made him

shiver. 'You haven't told Avozinha that we've fought, have you?'

'I'm not that cruel. I didn't tell her about the kissing *or* the falling out.'

He looked over his shoulder when he heard rustling coming from the house and spotted his grandmother packing her bag. 'I don't know which would be worse. And don't tell her this either,' he whispered at his sister, who shot him a grin before he got up and ushered his grandmother to the car.

He glanced at the clock as they drove, wondering if he would be able to see Eliana before his surgery. He didn't want the shadows of this morning haunting them throughout the day, and he needed to let her know he hadn't meant to sound as harsh as he had. That it had been no more than a reaction from the past.

He didn't know how to handle the feelings he'd started to have for her. For the family they could surely have together if they wanted to.

Diego shoved his thoughts aside as he went into the scrub room to change for surgery. Whether he liked it or not, the mayor's wife was now his patient, and she deserved him to be on top of his game just like anyone else.

Nerves made Eliana's stomach turn inside out as she settled down on the exam table. When she'd arrived in the obstetrics department the receptionist had asked her to go through to a room immediately. A fact she was grateful for. While her pregnancy wasn't exactly a secret, she didn't want to invite any questions from the staff if they happened to pass by and see her there.

She had told the receptionist to keep an eye out for Diego and send him through if he arrived, and was glad that she hadn't had to specify why she wanted to see him.

Dr Felix sat on a stool next to her, looking at the patient chart on a tablet in front of her and asking all the routine questions. Eliana answered them, her eyes darting back to the door, hoping that at any moment Diego would burst through it, apologising for his delay.

A small voice in her head told her that he wouldn't come. Not after the way they had parted this morning. But she ignored the doubt growing inside her, wanting to believe that he wouldn't not show up just because they'd had an argument. As co-parents, that would probably happen more often than they wanted. Would he always bail when they were standing on opposite sides?

That thought struck fear in Eliana's heart. The thought of getting to know his family—and getting to know her own family through him—had filled her with a warmth that made her heart beat faster. Somewhere along the line her feelings for him had become a lot more tangible than she had anticipated. Wanted, really. But would she even fit into his life? Did he want her to? Her intention to leave Rio remained the same. And Diego hadn't asked her to reconsider, either.

She had found a replacement chief of medicine. The lawyers were all but finished dealing with the estate of her father. After that she would be heading back to Belo Horizonte, leaving Rio and all its painful memories behind her. She'd need to forget about whatever feelings she had for Diego because they clearly were not meant to be.

She couldn't even count on him to come to the scan of their unborn child.

'Both you and the baby are in perfect condition, Dr Oliveira,' Dr Felix informed her, bringing her thoughts back into the room. 'I'm having a look at the results of your prenatal blood tests right now, but unless I see anything concerning you can just come back in a few weeks for your sixteen-week check-up.'

'Oh, I probably won't be here by then. I'm heading back…back home as soon as my business here is done.' She stumbled over the word *home*, her heart skipping a painful beat. She had grown more attached to this place than she was ready to admit.

'I'll make sure to send you a copy of your file so your new doctor has all the information you need.' Dr Felix smiled at her, then looked back at her tablet. 'Are you ready to know the sex of the baby?'

Eliana's eyes went wide with surprise. She had forgotten that they had done a blood test that would tell her the sex of her baby even at this stage. Again her eyes darted to the door, which remained stubbornly closed, and her chest constricted. He really wasn't coming.

Dr Felix noticed her gaze, following it with her own. 'Waiting for the father?'

'Yes, but I think he might be stuck in surgery.'

She didn't believe that, but it was a better excuse than the fact that he'd bailed because they'd argued and he didn't want to operate on the mayor's wife. The surgery must have ended hours ago.

'We can keep this information from you a bit longer if you want to wait.'

The problem was that Eliana wasn't sure.

Part of her did want to wait—desperately. Despite all the barriers, all the walls and traps she had set around herself, Diego had danced around every single obstacle and planted himself in her heart. She wanted him to be a part of this moment, to be a part of her family—wanted to share the highs and lows of her pregnancy with him.

But he had accused her of putting profit over patient care, just as her father had done. And to hear that he thought so little of her after all the time they had spent together had crushed her heart into tiny pieces.

Dr Felix had clearly sensed her hesitation. She picked up a small piece of paper from her desk, writing something on it before putting it in an envelope, which she handed to Eliana.

'These are the blood test results. You can open it together if you want to find out.'

Eliana took the envelope with a grateful smile and jumped off the table, pulling her blouse back into place.

As she walked out of the obstetrics department she grabbed her phone to look at the surgical plan for the afternoon. Perhaps Diego had been pulled into an emergency surgery...

Something was definitely off when Eliana arrived at the orthopaedics department. The staff's whispers died down the second she got close enough to decipher some words, and picked up as soon as she was far enough not to overhear their chatter. A pang of terror grabbed at her heart. This had something to do with Diego. She had known that the instant she had arrived, even though there was nothing to indicate that.

'Where is Dr Ferrari?' she asked a passing nurse, who looked at her with wide eyes.

'He's in the VIP room. It's the mayor's wife. She...'

The young woman's voice trailed off, and Eliana shuddered, her suspicions confirmed.

Something had happened during surgery.

All thoughts of him missing her appointment were wiped from her brain, all her attention immediately on the critical patient they had in their care.

Whatever she had feared finding in the patient's room, the reality was a lot worse than she had imagined. The sound of a flat beep drifted into the hall before she arrived, filling her with a sense of dreadful foreboding. A flat heart monitor was never a good sign. Neither was the fact that the room beyond was too quiet.

Eliana braced herself as she entered the room, analysing the scene in front of her. A female patient lay in a hospital bed, her chest cracked open in what looked like an emergency thoracotomy—something a surgeon would only do if they had no other option and other measures to stabilise the patient had failed.

What had happened that Diego had needed to crack open her chest? Blood clot? They were common in women her age and could happen at any time.

A junior physician hovered around the bed,

picking up the different instruments that had been used in the emergency procedure and putting them on a cart. And behind him, slumped in a chair, sat…

'Diego?'

His face looked hollow. With his head tilted backwards, she could see the blood that covered the front of his scrubs as well as parts of his arms, where the gloves had stopped. In the hurry of the emergency he didn't seem to have put on a gown for extra protection.

Eliana looked at the registrar, still fumbling with the instruments. 'Are you from the cardio department?' she asked. He nodded, clearly intimidated by the presence of the chief. 'Tell the head of Cardio I'll need to speak to her before we break the news to the mayor.'

She dismissed the young doctor with a nod of her head before turning back to Diego, who had sat up slightly.

'What happened?' she asked, doing her best to sound unemotional. Seeing him covered in blood had sent pangs of terror through her body until she'd realised that it wasn't his.

'Are you here to admonish me for letting your VIP patient die?' he said in a quiet voice, resentment giving his tone an uncomfortable edge.

Eliana remained silent, not rising to the bait he'd laid out. Instead, she squatted down in front of him to be on the same eye level.

Diego took a few breaths. Tiredness was etched into every feature of his body. She could tell that he had fought tooth and nail to keep his patient alive.

'My best guess? Pulmonary embolism. Even if we'd have caught it early, it would have been too late. I was about to leave when the post-op nurse paged me to check in on her.'

Eliana glanced back at the patient. That had been her first thought as well. A blood clot that had travelled all the way to the lungs, blocking off the flow of blood. She would have probably cracked the chest open too, and tried to manually aspirate the heart.

Looking back at Diego, she put her hand on his knee. The emergency had clearly taken a lot of energy out of him, and she suspected he might have tried even harder knowing the patient was important to her. Or did she simply wish that to be true?

Whatever the reason, the Diego in front of her looked utterly broken, and no matter how angry she was at him for missing their appointment, the part of her that cared for him a lot more than she was willing to admit wanted to take care of him.

They could have their difficult conversation later.

'Come on, let's get you cleaned up.'

She took him by the hand, and together they

walked back to her office, where she shoved him into the adjacent bathroom so he could shower.

Diego heard two muffled voices on the other side of the closed door when he stepped out of the shower after what seemed to be hours. He stopped, listening and trying to understand what was being discussed. One of the voices belonged to Eliana, but the other one was harder to pinpoint.

His question was answered a few moments later when he heard a third voice coming out of the speaker of a phone. The mayor. So the other person must be the head of cardiology.

Dread came rushing back into his system when he thought about the surgery. Hip replacements were routine work. Diego had done hundreds in his career, and his mortality rate lay way below the already tiny rate of hip fractures and related surgeries.

Low, but not zero.

Diego leaned against the door, closing his eyes as he shook off the thought of the last couple of hours. Losing a patient was never easy, but this one really bothered him—mainly because he hadn't even wanted to do the surgery, but had had to concede in the end that Eliana would have to ask for his time in such cases to garner support from wealthy benefactors.

It was something Marco had done constantly as well. The difference between those two, though, lay in what they'd intended to use the money for. Eliana wasn't lining her own pockets with the funds she'd drum up through such procedures—a fact he now realised.

He hoped it was not too late to apologise for his barbed words earlier today.

If only he could have given her a good outcome.

He'd let her down.

Diego knew this wasn't really true—that he had done everything he could to save the patient's life, and sometimes that wasn't enough. Despite knowing all that, he felt like an abject failure.

'You can come out now.'

Her voice rang a lot clearer than before, and a moment later the door opened. Eliana stood in front of him, holding a fresh pair of folded scrubs.

'I brought you some spare clothes.'

He took them with a nod of gratitude and slipped into the clothes before stepping into her office, where he stood for a moment.

'I just spoke to the mayor. He's still processing the news, but thank you for all the effort you put into saving his wife,' she said, and sat down behind her desk, pointing at the chair across from her.

Diego didn't take her up on the invitation but instead elected to stand, leaning his hip against her heavy desk. 'I'm sorry for how it turned out.'

'I know.' Eliana smiled half-heartedly and shrugged. 'He'll come to understand…just like every other spouse in such a situation.'

'Except he was more important to you.'

Eliana let out a sigh. 'He wasn't any more or less important than anyone else. There's a difference between rolling out the red carpet for someone and blatantly preferring them due to their status.'

'I know. I realise that now. And I don't know why I brought it up again. You don't operate in the same way Marco did, and I shouldn't have said otherwise.' He stopped for a moment, relaxing the arms he had been crossing just a moment ago. 'I apologise.'

His apology seemed to throw Eliana off guard, for she stared at him for a couple of heartbeats before finally nodding. 'Thank you. I appreciate that acknowledgement.'

They stayed quiet for a few moments.

Then, 'You missed the scan.'

The sharp tone in her voice was back, though he could see the restraint on her face.

The scan? Diego hesitated for a moment as the sequence of events this afternoon came back to him. With the urgency of the moment her appointment had completely slipped his mind. Guilt bloomed in his chest, mingling with the already heavy shroud of losing his patient. How could have forgotten about the first chance to see his child?

'Are you angry I missed the appointment? Ana, I had to attend the Code Blue of my patient.'

Eliana huffed, her eyes narrowing with a dangerous sparkle. 'I'm not angry that you had to see to your patient. What concerns me is that I had to remind you about the scan now. You didn't even ask if I'm…if *we* are okay.' She took a deep breath, seemingly steadying herself as she looked away for a second. 'I thought we were in this together.'

He paused. Her answer had not been quite what he had expected. She wasn't angry that he had missed the scan. She was angry because he hadn't asked about it.

'This isn't the last time I'm going to miss things,' he said slowly as he collected his own thoughts. 'If you take our kid away from Rio I won't be there for a lot of things. I want to be involved, and I'm sorry I couldn't make it this time, but you're the one carrying our child away from here.'

Diego's pulse quickened, his mouth suddenly dry as he stared at her confused expression. The truth of his feelings for her had started to coalesce—to the point where he could no longer deny it. He wanted her to stay—wanted them to be a family. Because he had fallen for her without even realising, and the thought of watching her leave hung over him like a dark fog.

'Diego…' She looked away, scrubbing her hands over her face. 'I'm still leaving as soon as my business here is done. I can't stay in Rio.'

'Why not?' He knew she struggled with her past, growing up alone and isolated. But was that enough to rob them of the chance of becoming a family? Wouldn't she try for him?

'Because there's just too much pain here. Even being back at this place brings unease to my stomach.' She lifted her hands, indicating the hospital around her. 'Everywhere I go I can feel the stares, hear the whispers about what Marco Costa did to my mother. I hear what a good woman she was or what a poor woman she was, depending on the person I speak to. That's all she'll ever be—a scandal. And that's all I'll ever be here as well.'

Diego's heart broke in his chest as the flood of words escaped her lips. Words she had spoken for the first time, judging by the sad but also strangely relieved expression on her face. So that was where her insecurities came from. She didn't believe she was good enough to be here, when nothing could be further from the truth.

'You've already shown yourself to be way more than the circumstances of your birth,' he said into the silence spreading between them. 'The mayor's wife just died in your hospital. You knew exactly what to do and you did it calmly. Like the true leader of a hospital would.'

Eliana scoffed. 'I wouldn't be so sure about that. Internally, I've been freaking out ever since I saw her in that room.'

'But you didn't let that affect you. Despite feeling overwhelmed, you remembered to care for the immediate family of the patient first rather than let yourself be carried away.'

Seeing the flaws in someone's actions rather than acknowledging every right step they took was something he was very familiar with, and he knew it took a lot of energy and self-confidence to snap out of it.

She looked at him with furrowed brow, digesting his words. 'I was never meant to be in this position.'

'You don't know that,' he replied, and reached out to brush his knuckles across her cheek. She didn't move away. 'Maybe this wasn't your plan, but neither was this baby—and look how that's turned out. You care so much for it that you want to carry it away from the place that caused you so much pain.'

His hand slipped down her neck over her arm and finally reached her stomach, where he rested his palm, fingers splayed across her abdomen.

Eliana looked down, taking a deep breath. 'You want me to stay?'

'I do, yes,' he said in a low voice.

'Why?'

His heart slammed against his chest as the truth rang clear in his head. 'Because I'm falling in love with you and I want us to try and have what we both weren't able to have growing up. We can be a family.'

It had taken him this long to realise that he wasn't doomed to repeat the mistakes of his past. Just because his father hadn't stayed true to his mother, it didn't mean that needed to be *his* life, too. He was free to love Eliana to the best of his abilities. Showing up to do his part every day. Choosing her and their child until the end of eternity.

Her eyes went wide in surprise, and he saw a slight flush colouring her cheek at his unexpected confession. Well, when he'd come in this morning, he hadn't thought they were going to have this conversation either. Hell, he hadn't even made up his mind whether to tell her about his feelings or if he should just let her go.

'Diego… I thought we had agreed to be friends,' she finally said after an extensive silence—and all the air left his lungs at once, as if someone had kicked him in the stomach.

Despite feeling utterly deflated, he managed a chuckle. 'I think we left the friend zone behind when we started making out whenever no one was watching.'

The blush on her cheeks intensified, and under any other circumstances Diego would have enjoyed the sight. If only she hadn't just rejected him.

An invisible hand reached inside his chest and squeezed his heart to the point of physical pain. Any more and he knew he would break.

'I'm not going to stay here,' she said. 'I can't. Not when I don't even know if you'll ever be able to put me first.'

'What? You doubt me because I missed this one appointment?' The accusation hurt in the depths of his chest, pulling the already suffocating band even tighter.

'No, I doubt you because you've kept things from me. Important things about your dealings in this hospital,' she said in a strained voice, as if she was willing herself to remain calm. 'But your motives are pure, and I've been working hard these last couple of weeks to give you the funds you need. I love how much you care about your community. But you're so used to doing things only the way you do it. I don't know how I would fit into that—how you see us as a family.'

She paused and shook her head.

'I'm not even sure you would have told me about the clinic if I hadn't stumbled upon Selma in the emergency department.'

Diego lifted his eyebrows. He opened his mouth to defend himself, but closed it again after a second of silence. Eliana wasn't wrong, and he didn't have any intention of stopping. Didn't feel bad about it either. Those people out there needed his help, and it wasn't *his* problem that the system was so fundamentally broken that he needed to resort to these tactics.

'I do what I have to do to help my people,' he said through gritted teeth, and saw her recoil.

'I'm not saying that anything you do is wrong. If more doctors were like you we wouldn't even need a free clinic. I just wish I could see the same tenacity in you when it comes to me and our child. But between your work and your mission I don't think we're as much of a priority as we should be.'

An icy shiver trickled down Diego's spine as he grappled to understand her words. 'You don't think you're a priority for me?'

The implication of those words shook him to his core. If his actions had made her feel that way, he really wasn't any better than his father. He truly didn't know how to be a part of a family, no matter how hard he tried.

His face must have shown the darkness of his thoughts, for Eliana lifted her hand to reach out to him, but stopped a few inches before their bodies could touch.

'I'm…sorry.'

He could see the conflicting feelings in her expression, and it was those warring emotions that almost made him believe she didn't mean what she'd said. But he had no choice but to believe her, even though he wanted the opposite to be true.

He pushed himself onto his feet. 'Don't be,' he said curtly, as the pain of rejection started to well up inside his chest again. 'Let me know about the baby. I can drive up for the next scan.'

He turned around, but stopped in his tracks when Eliana called out to him. 'Are you going to the dinner tomorrow? I've invited all the department heads to talk about the future of the hospital. I need you to be there.'

The future? Diego had rarely been less interested in the future than in this moment.

'If it's about work, sure,' he said with a throwaway gesture, before leaving the office and closing the door behind him.

CHAPTER TEN

THE DINNER WAS the last thing Eliana was in the mood for. Diego's unexpected confession had rocked her to her very core, and she felt the entire world had changed around her.

It couldn't be true. How could he love her when no one had ever done so in her whole life?

What had he been thinking, asking her to stay?

Her heart had been shredded into a million tiny pieces when she'd rejected him. Everything inside her had wanted to shout yes, to wrap her arms around him and never let him go. She'd wanted to be the kind of brave person who could forget about all the dangerous and hurtful things looming in the shadows of their romantic relationship.

His focus was so singular, she was afraid to find out what would happen if he fully focused on her, as she had demanded. But with the needs of his community, the grand plans he wanted to achieve, would he even be able to look out of her? For their child?

All the years of only depending on herself, without her father's love and support, had thickened the walls around her to the point where she could not trust anyone to come in. What if she let him in, let him see everything inside her, all the pain and chaos, and he realised what he was in for? What if he left? Eliana couldn't do that to her child—not when she had grown up on her own.

As much as she wanted to accept his love, to dare to hope, she couldn't be selfish. Her child needed her father more than she needed her lover.

Eliana took a deep breath, pushing the thoughts away. Tonight she had to be the chief one last time.

Her dinner for the hospital's department heads was being held at a restaurant Suelen had selected. They were to be seated in a private dining room so they could all talk freely with each other. But the first thing Eliana noticed was the empty chair and who it belonged to—Diego.

Her nerves lay blank from the conversation they'd had yesterday, and dread turned her stomach into knots when she sat down next to Sophia, who was looking at her with a degree of concern. Outside of Diego and the obstetrician, she was the only other member of hospital personnel who knew about her pregnancy. She also knew that it was Diego's child.

'I'm fine,' she said to the older woman, who had raised an eyebrow at her.

'Doctors make the worst patients—especially when it comes to high-ranking ones such as yourself,' Sophia murmured, her voice audible only to Eliana.

She smiled at the words. 'Thankfully, I will have you to deal with all my work very soon. Just send me an occasional email with updates—that should do it. I trust your judgement, or I wouldn't have picked you.'

'Should those emails contain a detailed Ferrari Report, or would you rather not read about him?' Sophia's tone was playful on the surface, but alluded to a lot more than Eliana wanted to discuss.

Was he not going to show up after her rejection yesterday, even when she had asked him to come?

Her mouth went dry and she reached for her glass of water, taking a big gulp. She had arranged this dinner in an attempt to reach out to him one last time—even though she was rejecting him she still cared for him, and she wanted him to know how much their time together had meant to her. How much she admired his indomitable spirit and sense of community.

One last gift for the man she loved but couldn't be with.

'I want to say that won't be necessary, but I don't want you to call me a liar,' she said with a sad smile.

'What happened?' asked Sophia.

Such a simple question, and yet Eliana didn't know how to answer it. What *had* happened?

'At the beginning we were just two people who met in a bar and never planned on meeting again. Until we got the news of my pregnancy from you. Then everything changed. We thought we could be friends but...' Her voice trailed off. But what? They'd fallen for each other when they really shouldn't have done?

Eliana still wanted to give in to his lure. She was standing at the edge of a cliff, ready to fall for him. But what if he didn't show up to catch her?

'For what it's worth, I've known Diego ever since he started working at Santa Valeria. He's a good man, and does great work with his pro bono efforts. But he takes himself a bit too seriously.'

Sophia shrugged when Eliana raised her eyebrows in a silent question.

'I don't know how to say it better. He just... gets too much in his head sometimes, and that leads to impulsive decision-making. It makes him a brilliant doctor in times of crisis, but

I'm not sure how well that works in personal matters.'

Eliana went quiet for a moment, thinking about what she had said, and then the waiting staff arrived with the wine she'd ordered for the table—excluding herself.

The twinge in her chest resurfaced as she looked at the empty chair one more time. He really wasn't going to come. It shouldn't surprise her—not after she had rejected his advances. But she'd really thought that he would come, for the sake of what they had and in spite of what they wouldn't have in the future.

'Thank you for joining me, everyone,' she said, and drew the attention of the room to herself. 'I guess I could have sent an email, but I didn't want to miss the opportunity to talk to all of you personally before leaving. As you all probably already know, I have finally made my choice for the new chief of medicine.'

She paused and raised her glass.

'I'm pleased to announce that Sophia has agreed to become the new chief of medicine and will usher Santa Valeria into a great new future.'

Glasses clinked all around, followed by a brief silence as everyone sampled their beverage. Eliana cleared her throat, suddenly feeling tight and constricted. She had practised these words believing Diego would be there to hear them, and understand their significance. Did it even make sense for her to say them?

'On top of that, I've also worked on establishing a more robust way of enabling you and your teams to help the less privileged communities here in Rio.' She paused to look around the room, her eyes once again resting on the empty chair. 'When speaking to you, I've heard many of you express interest in doing more pro bono work. So, starting immediately, a percentage of Santa Valeria's profits will be put into a newly established charity whose leader you can petition to release funds for pro bono projects. It will be led by Diego Ferrari,' she continued, and paused when she felt her voice wavering for a moment, 'who sadly could not be here tonight.'

Glasses clinked again, and Eliana sat back down on her chair. The cheerful atmosphere in the room was not managing to penetrate her gloom. But at least she had done something good while she was here in Rio, even if things hadn't turned out as she'd expected. With the new charity, Diego would have the right tools to keep going with his free clinic and help his colleagues bring in a significant number of cases from less wealthy patients.

She had done it because it was the right thing to do, but he had been the one to inspire her action. And now he couldn't even show up at the dinner.

* * *

'All right, this should be enough to hold you over.' Diego handed the patient a small paper bag with the required medicine in it and sighed with relief when the man closed the door behind him.

He let himself fall into the rickety chair behind the reception desk, burying his hands in his palms as he let out a groan of exhaustion. The plan had been to quickly stop by here and drop off some supplies someone had donated before heading to the dinner Eliana had organised for the leadership team at the hospital.

But when he had arrived at the clinic some people had already been waiting, needing to see a doctor right that instant. The patient they'd brought had been struggling with a nasty infection on his calf that Diego had needed to lance straight away, or he would have risked going into sepsis. By the time he had drained the fluids and packed the wound with antiseptic paste, hours had come and gone. But at least the patient had been saved and wouldn't lose his leg.

Diego glanced at his wristwatch, the weight of it still unfamiliar on his arm. He had worn it for the occasion of dinner tonight, along with a suit—the jacket of which he had tossed aside without much care when the patient's brother had hauled him in.

Just before midnight. There was no chance

they were still at the restaurant. Another emergency had prevented him from fulfilling the promise of his presence.

Maybe it was for the best. After all, hadn't he proved Eliana's point by skipping her dinner? When that patient had lain down on the table, a quick glance at his wound had told him the infection was severe enough that he needed immediate treatment and nothing else had mattered.

Should he have sent a message to let her know he was held up? The thought had swirled in his brain as he'd started the procedure, but he'd decided not to act on it. She would just see it an excuse after the way they'd left things. Hurt had stopped him from picking up the phone, and he had chosen instead to immerse himself in the urgent patient waiting at his door.

But he cared so deeply for both Eliana and their child. Hearing from her mouth that she didn't think he considered them a priority had thrown him into a dark pit.

Diego wasn't someone to give up. Ever. That was why he'd managed to keep the free clinic alive for as long as he had.

What was different with Eliana that he felt unable to pick himself up and fight? Their conversation yesterday had crushed him. He'd left her office feeling numb, as if walking through fog, trying to understand what had just happened. Why had he not stayed and argued more?

Because she was right.

Tonight would have been the perfect opportunity to prove her wrong, to show her that he cared about her above all else. But even though the thought had been on his mind he hadn't picked up the phone to get in touch with her.

Why?

Because Diego was afraid to feel how deep his love for her ran…how much it would destroy him to truly lose her.

Or might he resemble his father, after all? What made him think he could love her when he knew nothing about the concept? Fear paralysed him. What if he really was like his father? Maybe it was best she learned now before they got in too deep.

He pressed his palms against his eyes, willing his thoughts to stop chasing each other. The door of the clinic opened again. Diego swore under his breath. Had he not locked it after the patient and his family had left?

'We're not open right now, so if it's not an emergency please come back in the morning,' he said, without taking his hands off his face. Profound tiredness was digging its vicious claws into him, and he just wanted to rest.

'I thought I might find you here.'

Eliana's voice was coated with ice, sending a shiver down his spine.

He sat up straight, looking at her with a surprised expression. 'What are you doing here?' he asked, before he could think better of it.

'Me? What are *you* doing here?'

She looked at him, and there was a different kind of fire burning in her eyes than the one he was used to seeing.

'But of course you're here. Because you are Diego. You would give an arm and a leg to help your people, but you can't show up for me when it counts.'

Diego rose from his chair, meeting her gaze and not flinching at her bitter tone. 'I don't get to decide when emergencies come in,' he said, with a veiled expression. Agitation flared in his chest, mixing with the guilt he'd been carrying around since yesterday and creating an explosive fire.

'That's not the point. I was never angry with you for looking out for your patients. I know what it's like—I've been in your place.'

'*Have* you, though? Have you *really* been in my place? Have you watched friends die and families fall apart because of the inadequate health care that exists for people who live in the *favelas*? Because that's what I see every time someone comes through these doors. I clawed myself to the top from the very bottom so I could help them avoid such a fate. How could you possibly know that when you grew up in the best private school in this country?'

The words burst from him like a geyser that had been blocked by a boulder for far too long.

Eliana stared at him silently. The only indicator of her emotional state was the raised pulse he could see hammering against the base of her throat as she swallowed.

'You don't even know half the things I had to go through, growing up the way I did. I might have had plenty of food and clothes to keep me looking the part, but I was alone. You had your community to bond with and carry you through the hard times. I had no one.'

The last words came out as a whisper, and regret wrapped itself around Diego. He hadn't meant to throw his own internal turmoil at her.

'Why don't you tell me?' he said. 'You no longer have no one. You have no idea how much I—'

'No,' she interrupted him in a voice made from stone. She took a shaky breath, her golden-brown eyes trained on him. 'You do *not* love me. If you believe that I don't understand your pain because I grew up surrounded by my father's wealth, you cannot truly know me. I've told you so much already, but you still don't understand.'

Hurt was etched into each of her words—

a pain that resounded so intensely within him that it stole his breath. How had they got to this place where they had stopped understanding each other? It seemed as if the last few weeks had only been a mere dream of two people who were too different to tread the same path.

'Don't say that I don't love you,' he whispered, feeling the weight of her words settling on his chest and breaking his already crushed heart into pieces. 'I know it's true, whether you want to hear it or not.'

He might deny many things, but his feelings for her were genuine—even if they had landed them in this painful place.

'I thought I could do it,' she said. 'I really believed I could be in your life without hurting so much…without all this pain. But I don't think I can—'

Her voice finally broke, after wavering throughout her sentence, which prompted Diego to get off the chair and take a step closer to her.

She immediately shook her head. 'I waited for you at dinner, praying that you would show up despite the conversation we'd had. I wanted to be wrong about my reaction yesterday. I let you in…told you what it was like being on my own, having no one to trust.' Her throat bobbed when she swallowed a deep breath, her voice straining with each word. 'I asked you to show up when it counts—and you didn't. And you still haven't even asked about the scan.'

Her words hit him like a blow to his solar plexus, knocking the air out of his lungs as he slipped deeper into the dark pit he'd thrown himself into last night. After everything they'd discussed, all the things they had been through, he hadn't asked her about their child. He really wasn't any better than his father.

'I don't know what to say,' he rasped, his throat thick from the onslaught of emotions mixing in his chest. 'How is—?'

Eliana shook her head. 'I don't need you asking any more. I think we've reached the end of our road here, Diego.'

Her hand slipped into her handbag and retrieved an envelope. It looked bent, as if she had been carrying it around for a while.

'What is it?' he asked, flipping the envelope to examine its back. There was nothing written on it.

'Something you should know,' Eliana replied, with a rueful frown pulling at the corners of her lips. 'I'm leaving tomorrow. I know we have yet to figure out how we want to do things with the baby. I will be in touch as I get closer to my due date. But for now, I think I need some distance.'

'Ana, *por favor*...' He put the envelope down and circled the reception desk with two large strides, wrapping his hand around her upper arm as she turned to leave. 'Please don't go.'

'I have to—don't you see? Things shouldn't be so painful if they're right…if they're meant to be.'

She turned her head to look at him, and the pain in her eyes almost made him recoil.

'Maybe we were just kidding ourselves from the very start.'

'Ana…' He whispered her name and his hand went up to her cheek, only for her to flinch away before he could touch her.

'I have to go,' she said as they looked at each other, and she freed herself from his grasp, fleeing through the door before he could find the words that might persuade her to stay.

With a sigh that didn't even contain half of the pain and anguish welling up in him, Diego fell back into the chair and buried his face in his hands, his entire being crushed by what had happened in the last hour. She was gone, driven away by his inability to find her the space in his life that she deserved.

He was just like his father.

In the end, he had failed to be different.

A heavy blanket of sadness fell on his shoulders and he sat up straight again, his eyes falling onto the envelope he had put down as he'd tried to stop her leaving. He picked it up, turning it around in his hands a few times before opening it.

Inside he found a small flashcard with one word written on it: *Princesa*.

CHAPTER ELEVEN

DIEGO LOOKED AT the equipment being unloaded off the truck and taken into his clinic and felt the familiar twinge of regret in his chest. He had gone back to the hospital the day after that night in the clinic to find a summons to the office of the new chief of medicine.

There, Sophia had told him what he had missed when he'd skipped dinner—the announcement that he would oversee a new charity dealing with everything related to community outreach and pro bono procedures at Santa Valeria. It was a position he wouldn't have dared to dream of even with Vanderson in place. And Eliana had made it come true without even thinking twice about it.

Thinking about her still felt as if a searing hot dagger was being poked between his ribs, leaving him feeling hollow. Weeks had passed since he had last heard about her, although he'd tried to get in touch with her to thank her for the new job and to hear about their baby. His daughter.

That was the only thought that managed to pierce through the darkness he surrounded himself with, making his chest swell with unbridled joy and anticipation of the day he got to meet her.

A lot of the things said that night had been born out of fear—he realised that now. Fear of the unknown. Fear of trusting his heart over his head. Fear of losing the only woman who had ever meant something to him.

She alone had managed to sneak around his defences, making herself a cosy nest inside his heart. But his first reaction had been to treat her like an intruder, and the result of that reaction would be something he would regret for the rest of his life.

'Could you at least try to look pleased about this?'

Diego turned around when he heard his *avozinha's* voice behind him. 'I'm thrilled. With the extra staff and equipment we can service a much wider area of the Complexo do Alemão. We've even got our own patient transport van now.' He pointed at the roomy van parked near the entrance.

'You'll need to sound more convincing for me to believe you,' his grandmother muttered, while shaking her head at him. 'But you've been moping around like a sad puppy for the last four weeks. I guess you'll tell me it has nothing to do with Eliana and your baby girl being so far away.'

Diego sighed, rubbing his temples in a futile attempt to stop the emerging pain. 'I'm not moping. Am I sad she's gone? Yes, of course. I missed the first scan, and I wish I could be there for the next.'

Eliana had left almost four weeks ago, meaning she was well into her second trimester now and would soon have her next routine check-up. It pained him to think that he had yet to see his daughter, even if it was only through the screen of an ultrasound.

Throughout his life Diego had made many questionable choices and mistakes, letting the shadows of the past haunt him to the extent that it had sometimes immobilised him, rendering him incapable of deciding. It was that kind of primal fear that had made him stand back as Eliana walked out of his life for good.

'Have you told her you'd like to be there?' Márcia asked, and he scoffed at that.

'She's not taking my calls.'

'Can you blame her after the things you said to her? To think that you didn't even ask about the baby...' Avozinha clicked her tongue with a disapproving head-shake.

He drew his gaze away from the X-ray machine now being delivered to look at her. 'What? Who told you that's what happened?'

'You should know by now that your grand-mother knows everything. I really thought I'd raised you better, my *netinho*.'

Diego's ears suddenly pricked. Little grand-son? She had stopped calling him by that diminutive ages ago...only used it now when...

'Okay... I'm in trouble, apparently.'

'Of course you're in trouble!' Márcia raised her voice at him. 'How can you believe you are *anything* like your father? My son turned into a selfish and egotistical man, despite my efforts to raise him as a good person. But he used to be kind and sweet—qualities I see in you to this day.'

Diego stared at her, his mouth slightly agape. How could she possibly know that this was what he had been struggling with? That these were his innermost thoughts—the fear that he would turn out precisely the same because he hadn't been taught any better. But...

'He didn't teach me anything,' he whispered, and the revelation struck him like a ton of bricks falling on his head. 'He wasn't around enough for me to learn *anything* from him. He didn't teach me.' He looked at his grandmother in disbelief. '*You* did. You raised me to be better than him.'

Márcia shrugged, but gave him an encouraging smile. 'Glad you got there in the end.'

Diego froze, unsure what he should do next.

How could he ever have believed he would turn out like his father when that man hadn't spent enough time in his life to influence him? No, all the things he had learned had come from his grandmother and all the half-siblings he'd grown up with.

His mistake seemed so incredibly foolish now, and his outburst in the clinic a couple of weeks ago silly. He was in love with this woman—what else was there to know?

'She has her next scan tomorrow. If you leave now you can get to Belo Horizonte with time to spare,' his grandmother informed him.

He grabbed her by the shoulders, planting a kiss on her cheek before realising what she had just said. 'How do you know that?'

'Just because you were having issues talking to her it doesn't mean I missed out on bonding with the mother of my next grandchild.'

She said it so matter-of-factly that Diego had to laugh.

'Text me the name of her doctor,' he said as he turned around to leave, heading straight for his car so he could be in Belo Horizonte just after nightfall if all went well.

Eliana sat in the empty waiting room, softly talking to her growing bump. She had her hand draped over it, as if wrapping it in a protective cocoon as she waited to have her scan.

Even though she was well into her second tri-mester she had yet to feel any movement from her tiny daughter. A fact that—according to the several online pregnancy communities she had found—wasn't anything to worry about. Most women in their first pregnancies didn't notice anything until the twentieth week. Eliana was just past sixteen.

It was at moments like this, when her nerves got the best of her, that she wished Diego was here. At least she could have shared the worry with him, if nothing else.

The thought that she had made a mistake gnawed at her more and more. Their last en-counter had been charged with her fears—driven by them as she pushed him away and in doing that losing any chance of a future where they might have been a family. Where he might have sat here with her, holding her hand, as they found out more about their child.

And why? Because her insecurities had over-written sensible concessions in those moments. For her entire life she had been irrelevant, with no one caring where she was or how she was doing. The damage caused by her father's ne-glect ran a lot deeper than she'd understood be-fore she'd met Diego and got pregnant.

Because of her past pain she had demanded to be prioritised over things he didn't have any control over. For the first time in her life she'd had someone who truly cared for her, cherished her beyond any doubt, and instead of taking his feelings and actions at face value she had pushed him away—too afraid to deal with a reality where Diego wasn't going to abandon her.

It was an action that seemed so foolish now that she'd had time to process it. Why had she felt the need to leave Rio de Janeiro behind her as fast as she could? It wasn't the city's fault that her father had been a neglectful wretch. And Alessandro and Daria lived there—the only family she had remaining. Along with Diego's big family. All her daughter's aunts, uncles and cousins lived there, and so did Márcia, who was already more involved as a grandmother than Eliana ever could have hoped, and checked in with her almost daily. Not to mention Diego himself—the man she loved with all her heart.

Eliana had made a mistake, running away. She was at the point where she had to admit that.

Not for the first time in the last couple of days she took out her phone, checking flights back to Rio. She was still fine to fly, even with the pregnancy, though she'd have to choose soon.

Would Diego even take her back after the fight they'd had? Her heart squeezed inside her chest, sending a stabbing pain through her body.

She could sit here and wonder if he would, or she could go back and find out.

Her finger hovered over the flight, ready to buy the ticket, when the receptionist came into the waiting room to call her. 'Dr Oliveira, we're ready for you now,' she said, in a soft voice that sounded almost swoony. 'Dr Ferrari has just arrived and he's gone through. Your husband is...'

The receptionist waved her hand in front of her face, but Eliana's mind had gone blank after hearing his name so unexpectedly. *He was here?* Her mouth went dry and she suddenly felt both heat and chill rising within her, creating an intense storm as they met in her midsection.

She held her breath as she opened the door, and gave a soft cry when she saw Diego sitting in a chair with the sort of casual nonchalance she was so used to seeing from him. As if he belonged in this chair, in this place...

'Diego, you—'

He stood up from the chair and took a step towards her. 'I made it this time. No emergencies or last-minute patients.'

Her mind was still reeling from his sudden appearance, her lips parting without any words leaving them. She stretched out her hand, wanting to touch him, to kiss him, and tell him what a fool she had been.

But they were interrupted by her obstetrician Dr Porter entering the room, and after some brief introductions he started the scan and check-up.

Diego slipped his hand into hers when she winced at the chill of the gel on her stomach, and they both looked at the ultrasound picture in awe as Dr Porter showed them their daughter. He squeezed her hand as they looked at the screen together, feeling the magnitude of this moment. They had made this little life. Together.

'Okay, both mother and child are healthy and looking good. Have you experienced any discomfort? Unusual bleeding? Anything?'

Eliana shook her head, still speechless from seeing her daughter through the ultrasound, overwhelmed by the unconditional love she'd experienced at the sight of their child. Glancing at Diego, she saw he had a similar expression, and they looked at each other with a small smile, knowing each other's thoughts without having to say anything.

They walked out of the doctor's office and into the car park in silence, only stopping when they got to Diego's car. Then they turned to each other, deeply lost in the other one's eyes for a few heartbeats, before they hugged each other.

Tears started to coat her eyes, falling down her cheeks as relief washed over her. How could she have let him go?

'I'm so sorry, Diego,' she whispered into his neck, prompting him to take her face in both of his hands so he could look at her.

He swiped over her cheeks with his thumbs, brushing the tears away. '*You're* sorry? I have to apologise for *everything* I said. I was hurt and confused. I wanted to be with you, but I didn't know how. I lashed out. But if you let me I will try to make up for that for the rest of our lives together.'

'I thought you were putting me in second place. I couldn't deal with being part of a family. I didn't think I knew how to be with someone like you…someone who has radiance and love all around you. I'm still not sure I know how to be a part of it, but I want to try. If…' She swallowed the lump that had suddenly appeared in her throat. 'If you'll have me back.'

Diego looked at her for a moment, the brown of his eyes darkening. He looked like a predator that had just spotted its next meal. She held her breath as he remained quiet, then he dropped his head towards hers, brushing his lips against her in the kiss Eliana had been longing for since she'd left Rio de Janeiro a month ago.

'I love you, Ana. There's nothing in this world that can change that—nothing anyone can do or say to change my mind. And I promise to show you that every day until for ever.'

Eliana smiled as relief and joy collided in her chest, igniting the firework in her heart that had been waiting to explode ever since she'd met him that night at the hotel bar all those weeks ago.

'I love you, too—*ah!*'

She suddenly went rigid, and concern washed over Diego's face. 'What's wrong, *amor*? Is it…?'

But then she smiled again, even bigger than before. 'I can feel her… I think she just kicked me a little bit.'

Diego's eyes went wide in wonderment and he looked down, placing his hand on her protruding belly. '*Eita, princesa*, that's not very princess-like,' he said with a grin, and pulled her closer to him again. 'Oh, I almost forgot. Avozinha gave me this to give to you,' he added, and his hand vanished into his pocket, retrieving a small velvet box that he handed to her.

'She wants me to have her jewellery?' Eliana raised an eyebrow—and gasped a second later when she flipped the small box open. Her eyes snapped back to Diego, who was now kneeling in front of her.

'She thought her engagement ring would look good on your finger, and I think she's right. Will you let me show you how much I love you by becoming my wife?'

The tears she had just managed to get under control started to fall down her cheeks again as she nodded with a sobbing smile, pulling Diego off his feet and into her arms. 'Yes,' she whispered in his ear, and squealed as he wrapped his arms around her even tighter.

Eliana knew they still had challenges ahead of them, but whatever was coming at them they would deal with it. Together.

EPILOGUE

ELIANA FOUGHT TEARS as she looked in the mirror. The day was finally here: she was going to marry the love of her life.

She was surrounded by his sisters, who were laughing with her, and sharing advice from their own weddings, as well as cooing at her daughter Alice, who was lying in a small cot in the room, observing the proceedings through wide eyes.

She and Diego had debated for a long time whether they should get married straight away or wait for their child to be born. An urgency to tie the knot had filled them both, and neither had wanted to show any patience, but in the end Eliana had decided to wait. As a first-time mother she'd found the stress of pregnancy challenging, and she hadn't wanted to add to that.

The same day he'd come to pick her up in Belo Horizonte they had returned to Rio together, to forge a better future for Santa Valeria.

Eliana had been happy to leave Sophia to deal with the daily task of being the chief of medicine, freeing up her own time to help Diego build on the clinic, sharing the burden and the joy with him. She much preferred practising medicine over sitting in a stuffy office with endless paperwork. And bit by bit they were building the hospital they'd envisaged.

Now the day she had been so looking forward to had finally arrived, and she was sharing it with the people surrounding her. The Ferrari clan had welcomed her to the family with open arms, as if she were a long-lost sister, just waiting to find her family again.

'Don't cry! We've just got your make-up done,' Gloria said with a laugh as she put her arm around her shoulder, squeezing her full of sisterly love.

'Pick a random point on the ceiling and focus on it. That's what helped me,' chimed in Bianca, another one of the Ferrari sisters.

Eliana tilted her head backwards and looked at the ceiling above her head, willing the tears of joy to recede at the very least until they'd had all the pictures taken.

The door behind them opened, and all the women whirled around. Alessandro entered the room, followed by his daughter Daria, who was wearing the same dress as the bridesmaids.

'Is he ready?' Gloria asked, giving voice to the question everyone wanted to yell at him.

He nodded. 'I'm here to pick up my lovely sister and take her to the altar.'

The tears she had just managed to fight off started to well up again. It was finally happening. She was going to get married to Diego.

She took Alessandro's arm and let him lead her down the stairs, through Diego's *avozinha*'s house and into the garden, where they had set up chairs for the guests and a beautiful wedding arch. Her heart skipped a beat when the arch came into sight and the guests rose from their chairs.

And there he stood, at the end of the silver-white carpet they had rolled out, looking at her with an intensity she had got to know so well over the last year. His excitement matched hers as she walked down the aisle to meet him, her soulmate. Alessandro kissed her on both cheeks when they got to the end, before handing her over to Diego with a stern but warm look in his eyes.

'Are you ready for the rest of our lives?' she whispered when Diego leaned in to kiss her as well.

He smiled and grabbed her hand. 'Since the day I met you.'

* * * * *

*If you enjoyed this story, check out
these other great reads from
Luana DaRosa*

Falling for Her Off-Limits Boss

Available now!